By the same author

Shamar
Arrowdust
Wild Gold
Boneland
Roughshod
Torn Leather
Fury Street
Night Train to Utah
Dirt Trail Drifter
High Mile Rider

Riverbend Ransom

She must have been a woman of real class, Jonas had reckoned, when he first saw the dazed and dirt-scuffed woman being trailed along the banks of the Big Muddy by her captors. But his decision to follow and do what he could to set her free was to throw him headlong into a race against two equally brutal and determined forces: Eagle Neck with his marauding Cheyenne bucks, and the men plotting to hold the woman ransom against the biggest shipment of gold ever to risk the hazards of the turbulent river.

This momentous race would reveal a scenario intrigue, deception and rage. It would all end in violent showdown: a vicious riverside shoot-out. Le was destined to fly and blood to flow.

Riverbend Ransom

JACK REASON

A Black Horse Western

ROBERT HALE · LONDON

ISBN 0 7090 7104 3

Robert Hale Limited
Clerkenwell House
Clerkenwell Green
London EC1R 0HT

Typeset by
Derek Doyle & Associates, Liverpool.
Printed and bound in Great Britain by
Antony Rowe Limited, Wiltshire.

This one for R and S

ONE

The man watched intently through the grey morning light as the scouting party made its way along the mist-veiled banks of the Big Muddy.

Hungry Cheyenne, he thought, easing to the shift of his mount; Eagle Neck's bucks reconnoitring the likely grounds where a keelboat might founder on the swelling spring flow and prove easy plunder. Might get lucky too, he reckoned. Another few days and the river would be in full spate, with traders and the first paddle-wheelers out of Fort Bragg cutting a lively wash in the race to St Louis.

And it was a spit to nothing there would be the usual crop of mishaps and disasters: instances of bad luck, bad judgement, a greenhorn pilot misreading the river, a risk too far. Happened every year.

The man, a tall, weathered fellow born and raised deep in the Rocky Mountains and only ever known as Jonas, chewed reflectively on an unlit cheroot and continued to track the Cheyenne scouts' progress from his cover on the high bluff.

He counted six young bloods, fit and lean and

maybe a touch eager at the prospect of fresh pickings after a harsh winter. Eagle Neck and the main party would be holed up just short of Cripple Creek, keeping a low profile till the spring weather settled and the river tumbled back to life.

Meantime, the natural hazards were building up: treacherous chutes, snagged roots and branches, deadly sand bars lost from sight under flooding waters, deeper flows, hidden currents – and the Big Muddy bustle of boats and folk would find them all sooner or later.

Jonas watched the Cheyenne disappear behind a mist-furled knoll, eased back in the saddle, lit the cheroot and blew the smoke casually to the dripping pine boughs above him.

Time to move, he figured, head down the track to Cripple Creek, find himself some half-price rooming-house, wash up – maybe get to affording a bath – then eat, a steak, apple pie, sample fresh coffee, few shots of whiskey, sleep them off in clean sheets on a clean bed. Sounded good. Well deserved and not before time.

He grunted softly to the mount, rubbed its ears, planted the cheroot tight between his teeth and was reining away from the pine-screened view of the river when a blur caught his eye and the scuffing and cracking of twigs sharpened his senses.

He settled the mount again, shortened the reins and lapsed into a waiting, watchful silence.

The blurred shape moved on. A rider, tracking slowly, carefully, conscious of the scouting Cheyenne and in no hurry to make their acquaintance.

Jonas waited, unmoving, the cheroot burned to ash, his eyes narrowed to slits from which the light seemed to pierce like flame. He ran two fingers behind the mount's ears, soothing the animal's suddenly tensed neck.

More movement from the tracking rider, this time assured, beginning to relax, horse under a looser rein. And then a voice held low, but confident. 'Bucks have trailed downstream. We're in the clear. Let's move.'

Jonas held his breath at the sudden crack and scuffing of brush not fifty yards from where he had been watching the Cheyenne as three mounts were reined into life and moved forward to join the look-out rider. 'We head due north, upstream. Cabin's about five miles on, well short of Cripple Creek, hidden deep but close enough for keepin' the river in view.' The rider halted, waiting for the others to catch up. 'She holdin' on?' he asked.

Jonas swallowed, freshened his grip on the reins and peered closer. A woman among them, he pondered, watching carefully as the blurred shapes drifted among the tree shapes? His gaze tightened. Right there, between the two thick-shouldered riders. Corn-haired young woman, hair tied loosely into her neck, wearing a torn, one-time flouncy dress, more slumped in the saddle than sitting it. Looked exhausted from what he could make out of her face. Not keeping that sort of company from choice, he guessed.

'She'll make it,' said one of the pair flanking her. 'But I ain't for waiting around. Feel a whole sight better when we hit that cabin.'

His partner grunted and spat heavily into the

undergrowth, his glance flicking hungrily over the woman. 'Pretty as a picture, ain't she?' he leered. 'Even when she's all dirtied up like she is. Mebbe we can get to fixin' a bath for her at the cabin, eh? Yeah, mebbe we can do just that. Sure would like to see her take a bath. . . .'

'Hands and eyes off, Birdboy,' growled the leading rider. 'She ain't for messin' with. Too valuable. Worth her weight in gold in a few days' time. Don't you forget it.'

'Sure, sure,' grinned Birdboy. 'Just thinkin', that's all. Just thinkin'.' He hawked another heavy spit and winked into the woman's pale, sunken face with its dark, staring eyes and cracked lips.

'Let's shift before them Cheyenne get to nosyin' back this way.'

Jonas waited until the four riders had scuffed and clattered away upstream and the sounds of their progress faded to no more than the occasional distant crack, before he reached deep into his breast-pocket for a new cheroot, lit it and blew the smoke in a slow ring to noose a protruding branch.

He watched the circle of smoke break and disperse, then grunted quietly to himself as his gaze narrowed again.

The woman he had just seen head upstream with the three roughneck riders was captive. No prizes either for being able to spot, for all the unkempt hair, torn dress, dirt-smudged face, exhausted body, that she was a woman of class, maybe some wealth and substance, a whole sight more at home in some sassy hotel than on the dank, dreary banks of the Big Muddy on a morning when only scavenging Cheyenne and rootless drifters like himself were fool enough to be about.

And then there had been the fear in those staring eyes. What horrific prospect had the woman been looking into; who was she, where had she come from, and just how in hell had she come to be in the hands of two-bit scum the likes of Birdboy and his partners?

She was carrying a high price on her head – 'worth her weight in gold' – how high, and why? And who was going to collect, the scumbags, or was there somebody else waiting in the shadows?

Jonas shifted at the roll of the mount's flanks, grunted again, finished the cheroot, then gathered the reins tight in his hands. Apple pie, clean sheets and home comforts in Cripple Creek were going to have to wait. The look he had seen in the woman's eyes was beginning to haunt.

Two minutes later he was moving silently upsteam along the high ridge of the pine-shadowed bluff.

TWO

Jonas rode the ridge at the same steady pace for more than an hour, the Big Muddy swinging and dancing to the flow far below him, the trees, rocky outcrops and twisting shoreline coming sharply into focus as the sun burned off the morning mist and the skies cleared to a cloudless blue.

He had seen nothing further of the riders and the woman; they would have continued to hug the darker, shadowed track just above the shoreline, safe from prying Cheyenne eyes. Not until they neared the cabin would they break the pattern.

Whose cabin, he wondered, among the jostle of questions cluttering his mind, and just how difficult would it be for him to find it? And when he did, what then, damn it? A blazing Colt was hardly going to guarantee the woman's freedom, or his own future, come to that, not with three determined guns ranged against him. Patience, stealth, trusting to luck and some mighty slack security? He might get lucky, he pondered.

Jonas eased the mount over a sprawl of scree, waited for its feet to find a firmer hold in the dirt, and came back to pondering the question troubling him most.

The three men holding the woman were secondraters, run-of-the-mill gunslingers who might fetch up in almost any two-bit town, strutting the boardwalks outside some cheap saloon. Men who sold their no-questions-asked services to the highest bidder. Fast bullets, no scruples and little regard for their victims – save perhaps for Birdboy with his obvious eye for a female. He would not want a woman killed until she had paid her price for promised survival in full.

So, pondered Jonas, conscious of the day's first lift of sweat across his shoulders as the ridge trail passed through a shadowless glare, who were these scum working for, and why were they bringing the woman to a remote cabin overlooking the river?

The mount trailed back into the shadow of a rocky overhang and responded with a gentle snort as the man reined to a halt. Time to rest the horse, he reckoned, and take himself higher for a longer look at the track above the shoreline and whoever might still be on it.

Jonas climbed smoothly and quickly into the rocks, moving high above the river where its twisting, tumbling course carried it through a swirl of white water flows.

The track was no more than a smudged line of dirt wending its way through the pine growth like a sidewinder in a frenzy; a clear, uncluttered line where it broke cover in one moment, dark and virtually hidden from view in the next, its only pattern being to follow the river.

He settled in the rocks, adjusted his hat for the maximum shade against the sunlight, and peered intently at the track for the slightest, softest, most obscure movement. Nothing, not so much as a rabbit, a hare, a clattering bird. Might be hard pushed right now to spot a vagrant fly, he mused.

He licked at a beading of warm sweat, let his mind wander for a moment to the prospects of Cripple Creek, the pie, the bath, the cool beer at the saloon bar. . . . 'Hell,' he mouthed, jerking himself from the reverie at the first movement he had seen in what seemed hours. Nothing dramatic, barely noticeable, little more than the shift of a shadow moving from the cover of the pines to skirt a more open stretch of track.

Jonas frowned, concentrated his gaze on the shadow where it lay inert now as if merely another darkness among the trees. But not so. It moved again, sharper, more direct and purposeful; halted, waited, lapsed to being merely a shadow and was joined almost immediately by a second, and then a third.

Cheyenne. Jonas swallowed, cleared the sweat, blinked and brought his gaze back to the shadows.

Either a hunting party or scouts for a larger group, he guessed. The same group he had seen earlier? Had they got smart, played it shrewd, spotted the three men and the woman and doubled back on them, getting ahead with their knowledge of the terrain? He swallowed again. It was beginning to look very much like it, he thought, watching three more shadows slip clear of the pines and into position along the twist of the track.

Jonas tightened his lips as his teeth clenched. The Cheyenne were planning an ambush. Birdboy and partners must be close, trailing innocently enough into the hidden trap. Not that Eagle Neck's bucks would be much interested in the men. Their prize would be the woman who would almost certainly fetch a high price wherever they decided to trade her.

Cooking pot to fire for her, he grimaced, as his fingers strayed instinctively to the butt of his holstered Colt. Birdboy's grip to Eagle Neck's stranglehold was no prospect.

His gaze moved carefully over the pitch and slope of the land from his place in the rocks to the track. Plenty of outcrop stone and boulders, scattered pine and brush. He could hug safe cover until he reached the more open land, but then what: make some attempt to rescue the woman – single-handed against the venom of three gunslingers and a party of desperate Cheyenne – or warn Birdboy of the trap he was riding into, or turn his back on the track, mount up and go enjoy the apple pie in Cripple Creek?

There was little hope of the first possibility succeeding; Jonas had never been for turning his back on anything, which left him with some vague notion of warning shots from a hidden source confusing the Cheyenne and giving Birdboy and company time to make a dash for the cabin.

He eased his body against the steadily thickening heat, squinted into the high blue sky where a lone hawk circled as if in anticipation of pickings to come, and began to move slowly, carefully from his cover towards the track.

Jonas went like a shadow to a lunge of boulders, checked that the Cheyenne were still in position, peered hard at the track where it emerged from the darkness of the pines, listened a moment, tapped the butt of his Colt, and moved again, this time on all-fours as he buried himself in the scrub. Another pause. He swallowed on an already dust-dry throat, watched, waited, took a deep breath and headed for the next rocky outcrop.

The hawk continued to circle. The Cheyenne waited motionless. The man cleared the sweat again and blinked.

The darkness at the edge of the pines parted like a curtain as Birdboy, followed by his partners and the woman, emerged blinking and shielding their eyes against the sudden glare of the open track.

Jonas's gaze settled immediately on the woman. She was still slumped in the saddle, dirt-streaked, dazed as if drugged, but holding on by the thread of some deeper determination.

His gaze shifted quickly to the lurking shadows of the Cheyenne. They would wait until the riders were among them before springing the trap front and rear. Birdboy at the head would be the first to fall to a well-aimed blade.

He swallowed drily, his thoughts spinning for a moment on the satisfaction to be had in seeing the end of Birdboy, but the risks to the woman were too great.

He drew his Colt slowly, aiming the barrel high into the sky, counted down four seconds, then released a volley of blazing lead.

The high hawk screeched and spiralled through the glare. Cheyenne heads and bodies sprang above the brush and scrub like sudden growths; eyes flashed, searching for the gunman, narrowing on the curl of smoke.

The woman was jolted into sudden life as her mount bucked and pranced. The two riders flanking her tightened their grip on hurriedly shortened reins. Birdboy controlled his mount through a circling prance, his gaze wide and wild.

Jonas emptied the chamber of his Colt and began to reload, one eye on the mayhem erupting on the track. Now the Cheyenne had started to regroup, well aware that their prey, far from being taken by surprise, had gained the vital seconds necessary to realize the trap and whip themselves and their mounts into action.

'Ride, damn yuh!' yelled Birdboy. 'Ride like hell!'

The horses bucked, snorted, kicked loose dirt as the riders brought them round in a lathering of flying sweat and headed for the darkness of the pines.

A Cheyenne buck took aim with a rifle, only to have it plucked from his grip in the man's shot from cover. Another swung round, lips curled, eyes gleaming, his stare fixed on the rocky outcrop. He snarled, took a step forward, and screamed at the burning rip of hot lead into his thigh as Jonas's Colt roared again.

The high hawk continued to wheel; brush

snapped, twigs and branches cracked, whooshed and clattered to the riders' blind dash for deeper cover, the woman's mount being dragged, pushed and prodded beyond the Cheyenne's aim and reach.

Jonas waited until Birdboy's curses and the crashing had begun to fade before easing to one side for a sight of the track. The bucks had made no attempt to follow, and judging now by the way they were regrouping, pointing and talking animatedly among themselves, had no intention of doing so.

Jonas cleared the sweat from his face, settled a new grip on the Colt, and began to move. The Cheyenne, he knew, would have no trouble in continuing to track Birdboy and his party, but would they take the time to seek out the gunman who had sabotaged their original plan? Eagle Neck was a proud man and his young bucks were of the same mould. The mystery gunman would not be forgotten.

Jonas was mounted and trailing the ridge track by the time the Cheyenne had disappeared into the pines and the silence been drawn again like a curtain across the bluff.

But this time he was being forced to listen to it.

THREE

Birdboy would have something a whole sight more pressing than the woman's physical attractions to occupy him, thought Jonas behind a slow grin as he made his way over the ridge trail.

The scumbag and his partners would be pondering just how quickly the Cheyenne would take up the chase, but equally unknown would be the gunshots that had scuppered the bucks' intended ambush. Whose had been the finger on that trigger? Where was the shootist now; was he following behind the Cheyenne, they would be asking?

Jonas reined his mount into the cool shade of a pine bough overhang, came to a halt and relaxed. He scanned the high, cloudless sky where the hawk still drifted lazily against the burning ball of the sun, and wondered how fast Birdboy's progress to the cabin would be.

He figured for it now being somewhere around mid-afternoon, so did the riders plan on being holed up by sundown, or had their dash from the Cheyenne threat and the grimmer prospect of being hunted by them sent them way off trail and long behind their planned arrival? Did they have a deadline to keep? Would there be another party waiting at the cabin?

Jonas rubbed the mount's ears, flicked at a pestering fly and squinted through the glare to the track ahead. It began to slope away from here, running deep into the heavier and thicker pine growth of the shelving bluff. Thicker and deeper. . . . He pondered on the thought for a moment. One of the riders had spoken of the cabin being 'hidden deep' but close enough to the river to keep it in view some miles short of Cripple Creek.

He grunted and patted the mount's neck. Maybe he was closer to the cabin than he had reckoned. Could be he would have it located well before the light faded and night set in.

He urged the mount forward, his eyes following the hawk's slow drift. There was getting to be something unnatural about that bird's company, he thought.

The trail twisted, narrowed, pushed through thickets of scrub and meandered almost aimlessly into and out of brief clearings.

Jonas rode easy, relaxed, his hands gentle on the reins; only his eyes mirrored the telltale signs of his sharpened awareness. He watched for the slightest unexplained movement ahead and to the sides of him. He listened for the sound that was unmistakably man-made: the fall of a foot to dry brush, the crack of a twig, creak of a bough pushed casually aside, the sound without an echo that lapsed too quickly into silence.

Nothing so far, he mused, reckoning on the

hidden cabin coming into view in the next mile. Or maybe he would simply stumble across it, find it there on the next twist of the trail into undisturbed shadow. But how far was he behind Birdboy and his party? Would he be ahead of the Cheyenne? Was he even now being watched?

Would he, damn it, have been a whole sight better off keeping his head for apple pie and a bath in Cripple Creek?

His fingers twitched and tightened on the reins at the sudden slip and slide of a shadow to his right, but he kept moving at the same even pace.

A body, he reckoned, his gaze slanting to where the shadow had passed. Somebody lithe, supple, able to read the land as clearly as he would the Big Muddy racing away down there. Not one of Birdboy's sidekicks.

The shadow had been Cheyenne.

Jonas rode on, well aware that the buck would be staying close and patiently watchful, waiting until he was certain of the man's destination. And if it happened to be the cabin. . . .

He shifted in the saddle and leaned forward to pat the mount's neck – the chance to take a closer look ahead. All clear and quiet. So was the buck a lone look-out for the scouting party?

The Cheyenne had moved quickly and stealthily since the unsuccessful attack, already aware, it seemed, of the cabin being Birdboy's target. Good guesswork, or had the bucks tracked close enough to pick up a conversation similar to the one the man had overhead?

Jonas grunted quietly to himself. With the Cheyenne's sound local knowledge, he would wager the bulk of the scouting party had been settled at the cabin for some time; a runner would have returned to inform Eagle Neck of their find – and he would not be slow to see the potential – and a single trailing look-out posted.

He grunted again as if clearing an irritating dryness. The prying eyes of an eager look-out were something he could do without, he decided, bringing the mount into a shadow-dappled clearing and dismounting.

Seconds later, the fleet-footed shadow slipped closer.

The buck's gaze on Jonas's back stayed unblinking and tight, noting every movement, every shift of muscle as fingers worked over the tack, adjusted the girth and saddle, checked out the bedroll. Jonas hummed softly, as if welcoming the break in the shaded glade, relieved for a moment to be out of the sun's fierce glare.

The buck waited another full minute, then slid slowly, watchfully to his right, taking care to keep the reach of his shadow from his prey's sight.

Pause, wait, ease through a step. Pause again. The man was still humming, still busying himself with the tack.

The high hawk continued to circle across the cloudless blue. The sun burned; flies dived through it and headed for shade. The buck tensed, flexed his fingers, licked his lips, then launched himself like an attacking mountain lion.

His arms were stretched as straight and stiff as shafted arrows, the hands like claws tensed to dig into Jonas's shoulders, his eyes now suddenly narrowed and gleaming. The muscles rippled; there was the softest grunt of effort deep in his throat.

The clawed hands were within a reach of the man when he swung round, slapping the mount's rump to shift it in the same movement. The buck snarled, reached into space and began to fall as Jonas stepped back. The mount bucked and trotted into deeper shade.

Another snarl, this time on a gasp; a thud as the buck's body hit the scrub and dirt, rolled beyond Jonas's grab and came upright again, tensed for the next attack.

Jonas stared into the buck's eyes, but made no attempt to reach for his Colt, realizing now that this was going to be a hand-to-hand struggle. There would be no sounds save those from the bodies locked in conflict.

The buck sprang again, kicked out bringing a heel with a crack into Jonas's thigh. He lost his balance, fell, struggled against the slope, toppled backwards, aware of the looming shadow of the leaping Cheyenne.

Too late then to roll clear. The buck crashed across Jonas in a heaving gasp, his groans wafting on a rush of breath. Jonas's fist rammed home against smooth, sweating flesh. The buck grunted, fell away and lost his own balance in the sharpening slip and slope of the ground.

Both bodies were skidding, sliding away, crashing through scrub, limbs fouling on the twists of scrub, flesh bruised and bleeding from the grazings across broken pine boughs and barbed twigs.

Jonas spat dirt, blinked furiously, and was conscious suddenly of the swirling rush and drumming roar of the Big Muddy. Hell, he thought, grabbing anxiously at what seemed to be a safely rooted tree stump, how close to the river had they fallen? Were still falling?

The buck broke free of a tangle of brush, glared at the man, spat and drew a long, glistening knife from its sheath at his back.

'Sonofabitch,' groaned Jonas, realizing that his gun hand was clamped tightly round the stump and that, in any case, the blaze of a shot would almost certainly bring the other bucks from the shadows.

Nothing else for it. . . .

Jonas released his hand from the stump and forced the whole of his body to roll and squirm to the right, his arms and legs scrambling frantically for a hold, any hold, he could find.

The buck came on, his only focus now on Jonas's back and the target of where the blade would be buried. His arms rose, the blade flashed, teeth gleamed in a triumphant grin, but in the same moment his feet were entangled in the straying roots of the tree stump and he was careering headlong beyond Jonas to the swirling waters.

The Big Muddy swallowed him with barely a murmur.

FOUR

It had taken an exhausting half-hour for Jonas – finally to struggle back to the clearing, to be certain that the Cheyenne buck had not survived his headlong spin from the bluff to the Big Muddy, to dust himself down, call up his mount and take a long gulp of by now tepid water from his canteen.

He had continued to wait some time in the cooler shadows, watching them begin to lengthen as the fierce sun settled to the western horizon; listening for shifts and movements that might indicate other bucks were searching for their partner, and not least wondering how much further and longer to the cabin – if that, in fact, was where the track was leading.

He gave it a few more minutes, satisfying himself that he was still alone and the buck had not been followed, then mounted up and eased away to the pines.

How long, he wondered, before the body of the Cheyenne was washed up at Cripple Creek?

There was already the first creep of dusk when the track disappeared into thick scrub and Jonas reined his mount to a halt.

End of the line, he thought, dismounting slowly, his gaze narrowed on the thin twist of dirt. So if this was where the track ended, then it seemed reasonable to suppose. . . . He stiffened, shifted his gaze to the left, laid a calming hand on the mount's neck at the snort of a horse close by, no more than a few yards into the thickest of the growth.

He stepped to one side and eased towards the scrub. Difficult to move silently through it from here, but he stooped low even so and crept into the darkness. Another snort, the stamp of a hoof, soft tinkle of tack from a still saddled horse. One of Birdboy's party? The Cheyenne would have tracked without mounts, but how distant would they stay and for how long?

Jonas crept on, easing through the tangles of ground brush and scrub and the clinging boughs like a slow-footed animal. He winced as a boot cracked a twig, cursed softly as burrs snagged at his shirt, reckoned gloomily that if a Cheyenne buck decided to hit him now, he would have no chance of either defence or attack. He was a fly already in the web.

He had struggled another two yards when a shafting spread of the twilight brought him to a sweating halt and narrowed his gaze.

The cabin lay some twenty yards away – a dark, filtered bulk without real size or shape in this light and at this distance. His view was of the side that carried a small, dusty window and a tightly closed door. No sign of any life, not even the snorting mount. So Birdboy's horses, he figured, must be loose-hitched at the rear.

What of the tracking Cheyenne? No sign of them either. But Eagle Neck would bide his time; he was in no hurry, not when there was a prized woman at stake.

Jonas settled, one hand on a branch, his gaze steady on the cabin, probing for the slightest detail that might confirm a presence. Birdboy and his sidekicks would resist lighting a fire – sparse jerky and water for supper, if they were lucky – and they would not want a lantern glowing while ever they thought the Cheyenne close and watching.

Would they risk moving the woman again by night, or were they under strict orders not to leave the cabin? Jonas's gaze shifted to a new concentration on the cobweb-cluttered window. No hope of seeing anything through it, but there had been the occasional shadow seeming to drift across it.

Jonas licked his lips, grunted and relaxed. It was going to be a long wait till nightfall.

The movement came as night closed in and the darkness settled.

Jonas tensed as the cabin door opened on a stifled creak; at first no more than the merest chink, then wide enough for whoever was on the other side to see through the gap.

Silence. The door did not move.

Jonas's eyes ached as they tightened for a sight of the slightest shape. But nothing. No sounds, no light, no scrape of a boot, hissed words, hushed voice.

His gaze slid quickly to the vaguely outlined scrub and silhouetted pines, probing as it had for the past hour for any sight or sign of the Cheyenne. Still nothing.

The door inched on another creak, wide enough now for Birdboy's body to slink through the gap like a cat on a night prowl. He waited a moment, pressed tight to the cabin wall, one hand on the butt of his holstered Colt, the other closing the door behind him, the whites of his anxious eyes flashing on the darkness.

Five, ten, fifteen seconds . . . and then he moved on, stealthily, silently, edging to the side of the building before pausing, waiting again, reassuring himself that there was not a Cheyenne buck poised to jump him, and slipping quickly away, out of the man's line of vision.

Jonas calculated it would take even the cautious Birdboy no more than a minute to calm his horse, mount up and melt soundlessly into the night.

And the Cheyenne, if they were watching, would let him go.

Jonas swallowed tightly, conscious of a line of cold sweat beneath his hat-band. Eagle Neck's bucks would welcome the prospect of there being one less body guarding the woman. Their only concern was for her to be in the cabin. The rest, they would reckon, would be easy, in their own time.

Silence and stillness descended again. Jonas continued to wait and watch, impatient in one breath to be moving, aware in the next he had stayed undetected this far. He had the glimmer of an edge. Now all he had to do was get into the cabin unseen. . . .

He took a deeper breath, bent low and made his way to his left, stepping almost blind through the scrub as he began to circle the cabin, seeking out the areas of deepest darkness at the cabin door, realizing on a cold chill at his back that it was the only way in.

He broke cover on a sudden decision and burst of speed that brought him low and as silent as a shadow to the side of the cabin and within three paces of the door.

He watched, waited, slid to the door and tapped on it, his body numb with tension. Had he been seen? Was he being watched? Had the tap been heard by the sidekicks? Would it be answered?

He stiffened at the sound of a movement, the low hiss of hushed voices, the scuff of steps, creak of a floorboard.

Silence.

Another creak. 'That you, Birdboy?' clipped the voice.

'Who else?' croaked Jonas, in a voice that was barely more than a breathless whisper. 'Open up, f'Cris'sake.'

A bolt slid slowly. A latch lifted. The door opened on a gap just wide enough for eyes to peer through to the shadowed night. 'What's happened?' clipped the tight voice again. 'Why ain't yuh—'

Jonas's hand fell into the gap, fingers like claws on the timber as he pushed it clear of the side-kick's hold and slid into the room, his Colt already drawn and raised, the barrel whipping viciously across the sidekick's neck.

The fellow groaned and fell back, his body loose and limp under Jonas's adroitly aimed boot across his temple.

A shadowy bulk, the second of Birdboy's sidekicks, broke free of the deeper darkness and lunged at Jonas as if hurled like a missile. Jonas ducked, dodged, scraped an arm across a table, sending a bottle and glasses clattering to the floor – damn the noise, he thought! – and reached wildly for his balance.

The bulk came on, lost his footing, stumbled and crashed across Jonas's gun hand, forcing the trigger-finger into an instinctive reaction.

The shot was part muffled from a barrel already buried in the sidekick's heavy gut, the blood warm and sticky across the butt and through Jonas's fingers. 'Hell!' he muttered, pushing aside the dead weight and scrambling in a clatter of more noise to his feet.

He crossed quickly to the side of the dusty window, squinted through the clearest space, rubbed a finger through the cobwebs. 'Thank God,' he murmured on a hiss of breath. There were no signs as yet of the Cheyenne moving in for the kill, no sounds either until he heard the dry-throat crackle of the woman's trembling voice.

FIVE

'Don't come a step closer, whoever you are. I've got a knife, and believe me I'll use it.'

The voice, for all its cracked dryness, so brittle and frail it seemed it might splinter, had a tone of class and breeding about it, thought Jonas, peering intently across the gloom and shadows for a shape to the sound. The woman was no cheap trail whore and, whatever her condition, in no mood for messing with.

'Are you hearing me?' cracked the voice again.

'Yes, ma'am,' said Jonas, almost tempted to touch the brim of his hat as a courtesy. 'I'm hearin' yuh, but I figure you should know we've got about three minutes before a whole party of none too happy Cheyenne bucks hits this cabin like bad weather. So I suggest—'

'Who are you?' snapped the voice. 'Why are you here?'

'Folk generally call me Jonas – just that for what it's worth – but it ain't relevant right now, ma'am, and as for why I'm here, I been followin' yuh and the rats holdin' yuh since soon after sunup back there on the bluff. I reckoned you for bein' in bad shape, but mebbe I had that a mite wrong.

Seems like you're copin', so if you don't mind I'll
get myself—'

'No, wait. I'm sorry.' The voice was easier now, a
touch softer. There might even have been the hint
of a swallowed sob. 'I didn't mean. . . . Thank you.
I'll do whatever you say.'

Jonas stiffened, wiping his blood-smeared hand
down the side of his pants, his gaze narrowing as
the woman, still in the torn, stained dress,
stepped into the faintest smudge of light across
the cabin floor, laid a bone-handled skinning knife
on the table and brushed nervously but instinctively at a fall of tangled hair.

'Alicia Furneaux,' she murmured, tempted to
offer a hand, then thinking better of it.

Jonas nodded, grunted and turned back to the
window. 'We're down to one minute before hell
arrives, so you follow me, do as I say, when I say.
No messin', ma'am.'

'There are horses at the back.'

'No time. We head for mine and hope we make
it.'

'What about them?' trembled the woman,
glancing hurriedly at the sprawled bodies.

'Fella there ain't bothered, and never will be
again. The other will be sleepin' some for a while
yet.' Jonas stood away from the window. 'You
handle a gun?'

The woman's eyes clouded for a moment. She
shivered, hugged her arms across her. 'If I have
to,' she said uneasily.

'No time for lessons,' grunted Jonas, collecting
the dead sidekick's Colt and handing it to the
woman. 'You'll know how if you have to. Let's go.'

*

Only two things could happen; only one would, thought Jonas, easing open the cabin door just wide enough to see the silhouetted treeline.

The Cheyenne bucks could decide on a fast attack, risk the odds, grab the woman and melt away. Or they could wait, watch whoever left the cabin, track them until first light, and then attack.

Either way, they left Jonas with no choice.

'We move fast and low,' he murmured to the woman. 'Minute we're out of here, we keep goin' and don't stop for nothin'. Understand?' The woman nodded nervously. 'Good. Now let's try reachin' that old horse of mine.'

They were out of the cabin, the door creaking closed behind them, and into the gently moonlit night in seconds. Jonas's grip on the woman's hand tightened as he led her fast and low for the scrub and tree cover.

So far, so good, he thought, his eyes flicking first left then right for the slightest movement; the bucks were letting them run. It figured. They would track their prey without difficulty during the hours of darkness and much prefer taking the woman unharmed and still in one safe piece at sun-up. Meantime, they had the leftovers at the cabin to pick over. Only question remaining unanswered for the moment was, where had Birdboy headed? Maybe the woman knew his planning.

They had reached the horse and mounted up in what seemed then one breathless movement. Jonas eased the mount quickly to the track, this time putting his back to the river and the bustle of Cripple Creek and pushing north, high into the peak country where the pine forest thickened before shredding to a straggle on the mountain ranges.

'We made it,' sighed Alicia at Jonas's back, her arms wrapped tight around his waist.

'No, ma'am, the Cheyenne let us go. They're lookin' for an easier pickin' when it's light.'

'Picking?' frowned Alicia.

'Y'self, ma'am. It's you they want.'

'But that's ridiculous. It's an outrage. I have no intention—'

'T'ain't a question of your intentions, lady. It's Eagle Neck's figurin'. Now I don't know how come you managed to land yourself with the likes of Birdboy and company back there – we ain't come to that yet – but I sure as hell know the price them Cheyenne bucks have on your head right now, and believe me it's big and worth goin' to a whole heap of trouble for.'

'But they can't—'

'They can, ma'am, and will, and if we don't make some fast trailin' in the next two hours, you're goin' to have a painful initiation into their way of seein' things. So I suggest yuh hold on tight there and keep your eyes wide open. We're goin' to have company every foot of the way.'

'The way?' frowned Alicia again. 'The way to where exactly?'

'That ma'am, as they say, is in the lap of the gods.'

*

And so it was, reckoned Jonas, as he reined the mount steadily but inevitably higher through the hours of darkness. He knew the sprawling, teeming banks of the Big Muddy from the Rockies to the plains deeper south as well as he knew the stitching on his saddle. They had been his life for as long as he could recall, but the mountains were something else. Unknown to him and trailed only through the foothills. Even so, they were his only hope of staying alive and keeping the woman out of the Cheyenne and Birdboy's hands. But sooner or later he would have to come back to the river.

'Why aren't we heading for Cripple Creek?' hissed Alicia as the mount settled to a steady pace along the track.

'That scumbag Birdboy for one good reason, ma'am. Two bits to a dollar that's where he headed.'

'But there'd be the law there, a sheriff. We could have Birdboy arrested and jailed.'

Jonas grinned softly to himself. 'Men like Birdboy don't jail easy, ma'am. 'Sides, yuh can bet he was headin' to the Creek to meet up with somebody. No other reason for leavin' you at the cabin. Take it from me, Birdboy ain't workin' alone. He'll have friends, powerful, big time. They were holdin' you against a high ransom – am I right?'

Alicia was silent for a moment. The mount paced quietly, hoofs scuffing at the scrub and dirt, clipping eerily at a rock in the shelving terrain, tack tinkling softly. 'You're right, Mr Jonas,' she said at last. 'It was ransom.'

'You wanna tell me about it?'

'I owe you that much at the very least. Owe my life to you right now. If you hadn't—'

'That's in the past, ma'am,' interrupted Jonas. 'We got a whole heap of the present starin' us plumb in the face this minute, and not a deal of time to figure on shapin' up a future. You want either of us to come out of this in one piece, I suggest you get to some explainin', fast as you can.'

Again Alicia waited a moment as if gathering her thoughts from the nightmare of events. 'You expressed no surprise or recognition when I mentioned my name,' she began.

'That's so, ma'am. Can't say I've crossed it before.'

'You know nothing of my father, Oliver Furneaux? Obviously not. But you might have heard of the St Louis and Illinois State Bank. My father is its president. He owns it.'

Jonas swallowed tightly and flexed his fingers over the reins. 'Yes, ma'am,' he murmured hoarsely, 'I've heard of that sure enough.'

'A large – a very large – shipment of gold dust, tens of thousands of dollars' worth, from the gold mines in the northern Rockies is due to leave Fort Bragg about now aboard the steamboat *Ada Benson* bound for St Louis. Such is the size and importance of the shipment, that my father is aboard the boat to oversee the valuable cargo on its way to his bank personally. I was to join the *Ada Benson* at Cripple Creek where the boat refuels. My father thought a riverboat trip at this time of the year would be good for my health.'

'Kinda had his good intentions scuppered some,

didn't he?' murmured Jonas through a wry grin. 'What went wrong?'

Alicia gathered herself again from the twitch of a sudden shiver. 'Simple enough,' she began in the same matter-of-fact tone. 'I had been wintering with my fiancé's family at their ranch at Sioux Falls. My fiancé, Mr Harley Wensum, a partner in the bank, is with my father aboard the steamboat. I left Sioux Falls accompanied by the ranch manager by stage for Cripple Creek where we had accommodation arranged at the Palace Hotel and were to await the arrival of the *Ada Benson*. We never made it.'

Another pause, another tensed shiver.

'Don't tell me,' said Jonas. 'Birdboy and his rats hit the stage some remote place between the Falls and Cripple Creek, grabbed you, scattered the horses and left no witnesses. Right? The deal bein' to trade your life for that gold shipment bein' so conveniently watched over by your father and fiancé aboard the *Ada Benson*. Right again?' Jonas grunted. 'Lady,' he added, 'you are in one helluva mess – with respect.'

'If we could just get to Cripple Creek, talk to the sheriff, get him to jail Birdboy, perhaps somehow alert my father. . . .' Alicia's voice cracked and faded. She shivered again and tightened her grip round the man's waist.

'I hadn't been for plannin' on meetin' up with the daughter of the president of a state bank,' said Jonas quietly, 'specially not in these circumstances. T'ain't my normal run of days, but seein' as I have, I reckon you'd best get to figurin' who it is, ma'am, who happens to know precisely the details of that gold shipment and its journey, and just as precisely where you were headin' and when. And that ain't in Birdboy's range of mental abilities believe me.'

Jonas flicked the reins. 'And while you're ponderin' on that, I'll just be keepin' a watch on the two bucks back there in the scrub who ain't showin' the slightest sign of goin' home for breakfast!'

SIX

The bucks were still there, still tracking the slow-going mount and its weary riders at a safe, shadowy distance, an hour later when Jonas eased the horse into a deeper cover of pines and halted.

'Why are we stopping?' hissed Alicia at Jonas's back. 'Is it safe?'

No, ma'am, it ain't,' he murmured, dismounting. 'Far from it. And it's beginnin' to get like a burr in the boot – irritatin'.'

Alicia frowned as she fell into his steady hold and stumbled for her balance.

'Easy there, miss. Goin' to take a while for you to feel yourself. You ain't been keepin' good company.'

Alicia Furneaux tossed her hair, straightened and dusted the creased and tattered dress as if about to make an entrance, and glanced anxiously round her. 'They're still there, aren't they? The Cheyenne. I can feel their eyes on me.'

'Oh, they're there all right,' said Jonas, busying himself unnecessarily with the tack and bedroll. 'Never left us, and one of 'em won't. The other will make off back to report to Eagle Neck come first

39

light. That's the bit that bothers me.'

'You can't fight them both,' hissed Alicia. 'That would be impossible, not to say ridiculous.'

Jonas's stare, piercing again as if suddenly torched into flame, settled in her eyes. 'Yuh reckon?' he drawled. 'Well, mebbe I'm goin' to need some help.'

'You surely don't expect me—'

'Fancy winterin' on a ranch out Sioux Falls and life in some dude place back at St Louis mebbe don't equip yuh none for the banks of the Big Muddy and tacklin' a bunch of greedy-eyed Cheyenne, but you're sure as hell goin' to learn fast how to set about it – beginnin' now.' Jonas's stare burned on. 'That, lady, or kiss Cripple Creek, yuh pa, fiancé and St Louis goodbye. Yuh seem to have a simple choice and right now – with all due respect to yuh, Miss Furneaux – I ain't much for debatin' it. We ain't got the time.'

Alicia blinked, her lower lip trembled, but only once, as she wiped hurriedly at her eyes and tossed her hair in a show of confidence. 'Yes, of course,' was all she said, her gaze firmer on Jonas's face.

He turned back to the mount and began to untie the bedroll, speaking fast and low as his fingers worked. 'I got a spare shirt and pair of pants in this roll – not the best, but good enough – so you get yourself out of that frills and lacy fandangle you're wearin' and into these, and you do it right here, ma'am, in full view of what'll fast become two very intrigued Cheyenne bucks. And take your time about it.'

He was conscious of Alicia's stifled gasp and

collapsing expression as he extracted the clothes from the roll and handed them to her.

'I'm not sure. . .' she began, taking the shirt and pants in an already shaking hand. 'I mean—'

'Yuh don't mean nothin', ma'am, you do it. I'll be out there, in the scrub. Get it?'

'But suppose—'

But Jonas had replaced the bedroll, loose-hitched the mount and disappeared into the trees before Alicia Furneaux's bewildered gaze had blinked back into focus.

The night was still lurking through those slow hours before the first light from the east begins to break – and there was just sufficient now, Jonas decided, for him to detect already the blurred shapes of the Cheyenne.

They had closed in the minute the horse had been reined up and the riders dismounted, one slipping into the deep scrub to the right of the clearing, the other to the left where the twisted branches of a fallen pine gave him tight cover.

They had shifted a yard closer on the disappearance of Jonas, but shown no inclination to follow. Their prize, when the time came, was there and in full view. The woman was all that mattered. She would bring much wealth to Eagle Neck and his followers. A prize to be guarded with their lives.

Jonas grunted quietly to himself and slid away towards the nearest of the bucks. He could move round to the back of him with ease, he reckoned, providing he could trust to Alicia to play her part in holding the bucks' concentration. He could think of a dozen two-bit bar girls who would handle the situation without blinking; a St Louis bank president's classy daughter was something else.

He moved on, step by careful step, pausing only to peer through the grey-black gloom to check that the bucks were still in position and Alicia beginning to hold their attention.

She was taking her time getting started, damnit. Leave it too long and the bucks would get suspicious, get to wondering where the man had gone, why he had left her. Cheyenne bucks were quick to start twitching when tracking a prize.

The buck immediately ahead of Jonas began to turn, looking carefully, curiously round him, forcing Jonas to duck hurriedly, catch his breath and curse quietly under it. If the buck signalled to his partner. . . .

Hell, woman, get on with it!

Alicia Furneaux had stood uncertain and trembling for long minutes, in one moment staring at the worn pants and shirt as she might something she was about to trash, in the next glancing furtively into the trees, scrub and shadows, imagining the flash and glare of eyes, the look on hungry faces; seeing Cheyenne in every plunge of darkness, the leering gleam of Birdboy's grin behind every tree.

The approaching dawn air was thin and chill, her flesh a mass of what seemed like something creeping.

She trembled again, shrugged her shoulders, unfurled the shirt and pants and dropped them to the ground. Then, with a resigned sigh and toss of her hair, began to peel the dress from her body.

Jonas's fingers slid expectantly over the cool butt of his holstered Colt, his eyes narrowing to tight concentration on the shape of the buck snuggled deep in the scrub.

This one would have to be taken out soundlessly, he mused, the fingers flexing and then slipping clear of the weapon. No shooting, not here, not now. He licked his lips, conscious of a beading of icy sweat, and inched towards the shape, one eye flicking to Alicia shivering clear of the dress. Easy does it there, lady, he thought, the bucks are beginning to get interested.

He slid to the left, to the right, came on, each move trusting as much to luck as instinctive stealth, but he was closing fast on the buck whose body was tensed and transfixed by the sight of the woman emerging from the furls and folds of the dress like a butterfly.

One more shift, another yard. The distance faded as if dropped into a hole as Jonas reached for the Cheyenne's neck. Both men grunted, one out of the sheer effort of the grip of fingers on flesh, the other out of surprise and the sudden struggling to be free.

They fell back to the entwining snags and tangling whip of the scrub, Jonas's only concern now to keep the buck from crying out to his partner.

The buck's strength seemed then to harden – molten muscle one moment, iron limbs the next

– as he turned, twisted, squirmed, lashed out, one
hand flat as a frypan, the other tight as rock, the
fingers clenched, knuckles white hot in his anger.

Jonas thrust a knee deep into the buck's groin,
stifled the gasp with a hand that slapped across
his mouth like a mudslide, and thrust again. The
buck weakened, vomited, his eyes glazing and
then bulging as Jonas's fingers settled and tightened at his throat and slowly, deliberately began
to throttle away the lifegiving breath.

Jonas rolled clear of the body in a lather of
sweat, the few minutes it had taken to begin and
end the attack seeming like hours. He swallowed,
swished the sweat and loose brush from his face,
winced at the stabbing pains through his arms
and legs, and struggled to his knees.

He saw the dress first, discarded like crumpled
paper to the scrub, the pants and shirt alongside
it, then the second Cheyenne buck, his arms
locked round the woman as he dragged her, kick-
ing and screaming, towards the darkness of the
trees on the far side of the clearing.

'Hell!' cursed Jonas, struggling to his feet, one
hand dropping instinctively to the butt of his Colt.
His gaze narrowed, tightened. Rushing the buck
would be too risky. The Cheyenne would simply
draw the sheathed knife in his belt and lay its
deadly blade across Alicia's throat. He might not
kill her, but a few expert slashes across her body
would do all the damage necessary.

Jonas drew the Colt slowly, deliberately, taking
the weight and balance naturally in his grip. A
shot, at this distance at a target about as slippery
as a writhed rattler would be taking some chance.

But he was going to take it, anyhow.

Alicia was still struggling, her elbows jabbing, bare arms and legs flashing in their fight, eyes wild and bulging under the pressure of the buck's hand clamped tight across her mouth.

Only a matter of seconds now before they reached the trees where the strengthening first light had not yet reached. They would be gone, fading shadows, in the blink of an eye.

Jonas levelled the Colt, steadied his arm, relaxed his fingers for a moment, renewed the grip, took the pressure, held his breath.

The single shot exploded across the early dawn like the splintering of a slab of granite, the roar of it clattering a bird into squawking life, lifting a snort from the loose-hitched mount before echoing high above the treeheads.

The buck seemed to hang suspended for a moment, his face turned to Jonas, eyes wide and fiery, the hole in his temple trickling a dark line of blood.

Jonas stepped over the body, crouched at the woman's side and spread the shirt across her trembling shoulders.

SEVEN

'Just get me back to the river, to Cripple Creek, as soon as you can. That is all I ask, Mr Jonas, and I would like to set about it now. Right now.'

Alicia Furneaux hugged herself into the patched, ill-fitting shirt and stared defiantly through the spreading dawn light.

'I am grateful for what you have done and the risks you have taken – incredibly grateful, and I owe my life to you – but enough is enough. I cannot take any more. Get me to the Creek, to the sheriff. I will see that you are handsomely rewarded for your time and trouble, be sure of that, and then you are quite free to go about whatever your business happens to be. You are under no obligations. I shall manage, and await the arrival of my father at the Palace Hotel under the protection of the law.'

The woman fingered the collar of the shirt, pulled the front folds together where two buttons were missing, patted her hair and continued to stare at Jonas's back.

'It isn't too much to ask, is it?' she said frowning.

'No, ma'am,' said Jonas, turning to face her, 't'ain't too much to ask, but t'ain't exactly smart either.'

Alicia tossed her hair. 'Really? I don't see it like that, not after all this.' She glanced back to the dead body of the buck and shivered. 'You used me as bait, Mr Jonas. Nothing more, nothing less. Just bait.' She shivered again and grimaced. 'I felt like an animal, something penned, nothing better than a cheap lure. It was disgusting.' She glared at Jonas, her eyes glazed, angry, wet.

Jonas stared back without blinking. 'We trail out of here for them higher peaks up there,' he said flatly. 'We'll have mebbe two hours' start before Eagle Neck's bucks come lookin' for the pair we've just taken out. Oh, yes, ma'am, *we've* taken out. We did it together and we're still breathin' – but we're sure as hell, beggin' your pardon, carryin' a price on our heads. Big time. So now you figure on holin' up at Cripple Creek – assumin' you get there; assumin' Eagle Neck's fool enough to *let* you get there.'

Jonas turned back to his saddle-bag, his gaze coldly flat. 'You wouldn't survive one hour in Cripple Creek, ma'am, and that's fact. Birdboy and whoever he's workin' for would have you snaffled away and held tight in no time. You'd be walkin' like a fly into the web. And the law yuh keep referrin' to wouldn't lift a finger. About the only thing Cripple Creek's Sheriff Calpott's capable of is liftin' a full bottle of cheap whiskey. That he will do gladly.'

Alicia bit at her lip, stiffened her shoulders on the toss of her hair and folded her arms dramatically. 'And what, therefore, assuming you are right, do you suggest, Mr Jonas? You do have a suggestion, I take it?'

'Oh, yes, ma'am, I got a suggestion sure enough. Two suggestions, in fact.'

'I'm waiting,' clipped Alicia, a gleam flashing in her eyes. 'Anxiously!'

Jonas grunted quietly at the package he held in his hands. 'Straight jerky and canteen water – the best I can do. No fire. Smoke'd be spotted miles off. But we need to eat, ma'am, if we're goin' to have the strength for what we got facin' us. That's the first thing we gotta do.

'Second: for the heist of the gold shipment you described to be successful, there's got to be somebody aboard the *Ada Benson* working with Birdboy and the rattlers nestin' in Cripple Creek. So, I figure for us gettin' aboard that steamboat before it fuels up at the Creek. Without you in their hands, the rats ain't got nothin' to bargain.'

Alicia's smile was wry and a touch mocking. 'And you can do this?' she said. 'Get us off this bluff, down to the river and aboard the *Ada Benson*? You consider this feasible? Frankly, Mr Jonas, it seems to me more like a fit of madness!'

Jonas shrugged and tossed the package from hand to hand. 'Your choice, lady.'

'Is there one?'

'Not really, not the way I see it.'

Alicia unfolded her arms slowly. 'Just who are you, Mr Jonas? What do you do? Where did you come from?'

'Try the jerky, ma'am,' said Jonas, offering the package.

*

They left the pines and the scrub on a dirt track twisting into rocks and boulders as the light broke fitfully in the east.

Their early progress was slow but steady. Jonas had no good reason to tire the already weary mount too soon; he had an edge over Eagle Neck, and he needed time now to reckon on his approach to the Big Muddy and ask himself once again how it was he had become this involved, this deep, this committed, risking both his own and the woman's life, when all Alicia Furneaux wanted was a sight of Cripple Creek, and maybe the chance to buy her safety. And all he had ever wanted all those hours back was apple pie, clean sheets and a night's rest in a real bed.

The answers were harsh, hard, and might well prove fatal.

Jonas grunted quietly as the womans' head lolled across his shoulders. Her anger, sparked by her fear, had passed into exhaustion, her defiance subsided in the sharp realization that the situation could not be bought and buried. What had happened had been cruelly real; what was happening now was real, and the prospects in the hours to come were no flight of fancy. The real world had hit Alicia Furneaux like a thunder clap.

So maybe he should do just as she wanted: deliver her into the hands of Sheriff Calpott at Cripple Creek and let the so-called 'law' take over. Some chance, he thought. Calpott would probably be as anxious and greedy-eyed as any scumbag to realize whatever he could on the daughter of a St Louis bank president, moreso when he got to hear – as he probably already had – of the woman's connection with the *Ada Benson's* valuable cargo.

The 'law' in Cripple Creek shifted like the slip of a fickle wind: you went with whatever way it was blowing on that particular day, or against it if it suited. Not even Alicia Furneaux would be able to buy her way through that.

No, Jonas resolved, he would do the only thing he could do – deliver Alicia to her father and fiancé aboard the steamboat. And he was going to have only one chance. It would come where the Big Muddy deepened on a slow meander at Riverbend Pass. Miss the *Ada Benson* there, he grunted on the thought, and the future would be of no importance.

He reined the mount directly west, eased his shoulders against the woman's sleeping weight and flicked his glance quickly to the higher reaches of rocks and boulders where the slow curl of smoke from a gulch fire turned on the soft breeze.

Not Cheyenne, he decided, and definitely not Birdboy and his sidekicks. Drifters, trappers moving out of the Rockies to the warmer spring slopes?

How many? Had they been watching his progress from the pines? Would they show any interest?

'Howdy,' growled the voice, behind the priming snap of a Winchester.

EIGHT

He appeared from the shadows of the rocks like a shuffling bear, a squat, flat-footed fellow dressed in a vast shaggy-haired coat that buried his neck and reached to his ankles. His face, what could be seen of it, was just as hairy, grimy, pitted and gleaming through the scrub of a matted beard. His lips slapped over wet gums where a single tooth glinted like an ivory tusk.

'Been watchin' yuh some whiles,' he oozed, on another slap of the lips. 'Horse there looks a mite whacked. Two up ain't to be recommended in this terrain.' His eyes, glazed as pebbles in a pool beneath the overhang of bushy brows, began to narrow to a tight probe as he peered beyond Jonas to the stirring woman. 'That some female yuh got there, mister?'

Jonas sat easy, his hands seemingly lazy on the reins. 'A lady,' he murmured, his gaze shifting around the man like a light. 'She could sure as damnit use some coffee if that's what your friend's brewin' up back there on your fire.'

'My partner, Duckback,' slapped the man. 'He ain't much for company.' He continued to stare at Alicia as she raised her head, blinked, stiffened

51

with surprise at the sight of the man and the Winchester and tightened her grip on Jonas. 'She available?'

'Available?' frowned Jonas.

'Sure, available. We ain't had a woman in these parts close on a full twelve months.'

'She ain't available,' clipped Jonas quickly. 'Paid good money for her in Cripple Creek.' He felt Alicia stiffen behind him. 'Headin' up country,' he added.

'Not like that yuh ain't,' grinned the man. 'That horse ain't got another five miles in it with the pair of you mounted.' He slapped his lips, rolled his tongue over the glinting tusk, and spat decisively. 'Trade yuh a good-lookin' horse I got hitched back there for the woman. Sound teeth, bright eye, shifts like the wind when you've a mind. What yuh say?'

Jonas was conscious of Alicia's hot, angered breath on his neck, the bite of her fingernails through his shirt. He could imagine the look on her face.

'You wanna think it through?' grinned the man. 'Sure yuh do. Do it over some fresh coffee, eh?' The lips slapped and oozed; the tusk seemed to grow; a trickle of saliva dribbled into the matted beard. 'Get yuh down there, mister. Give that old nag a rest.'

Jonas grunted and slid from the saddle, then turned to reach for Alicia. 'I'm warning you, Mr Jonas,' she hissed indignantly, 'if you so much as—'

'Just leave this to me, right?' grunted Jonas.

' 'Course,' dribbled the man, probing the

Winchester into space, 'I ain't for tradin' 'til I've inspected the goods. Only fair, ain't it? You get to see the horse, I get to see the woman.'

Jonas avoided Alicia's gaze as he helped her to the ground.

Shaggy-coat's partner, Duckback, was taller, thinner, with large tinplate hands, a pinched, whiskered face, tight lips, staring eyes, the left one part hooded and flickering constantly as if beating off a plague of midges.

He lounged uncomfortably on the far side of the slow-burning fire where a pot of coffee simmered quietly, the smoke curling, twisting against the shift of the thin morning air. He looked up, but stayed silent at the approach of his partner, Jonas and the woman.

'Look yuh here, Duckback,' grinned Shaggy-coat, still probing the Winchester into space. 'Ain't this a sight for them sore eyes of yours? A real live woman. Now yuh ain't seen one of them in a whiles, have yuh? And ain't she some looker, eh? Touch of real class there.'

Alicia Furneaux shivered, tensed, then folded her arms across the ill-fitting shirt. Jonas watched the men, particularly the lounging, voiceless Duckback and his overworked right eye.

'My partner don't say a deal,' began Shaggy-coat again, 'but he sure as hell thinks plenty.' He turned to him. 'We got a deal goin' here, Duckback: the black mare for the woman. What yuh reckon?'

Duckback spat into the dirt.

'That's his way of sayin' he agrees,' grinned Shaggy-coat. 'So let's have some coffee, eh? Hell, ain't this promisin' to be one almighty, sonofabitch day – yessir, say that again!'

Shaggy-coat had smiled broadly, raised his arms and the Winchester in a whoop of satisfaction and thrown back his head as he kicked into a boot-thumping, coat-swirling jig that turned him into a stomping woolly mammoth – and in the next moment, a lip-curling, hissing rattler, crouched and threatening, the rifle in a levelled aim at Jonas and the woman.

'Yeah,' he snarled, eyes flashing, just one helluva day; 'ceptin' I ain't for partin' with the black mare there, but I sure as hell want the woman.'

Alicia gasped, stiffened, her arms unfolding to a protective hug around herself. Jonas simply watched, hands easy, eyes narrowed.

Duckback spat again. 'Yuh goin' to kill him?' he drawled.

'I'm goin' to do just that, my friend,' grinned Shaggy-coat. 'Precisely that. So you just give an eye to the woman while I get to it. This ain't goin' to take no more than a spit and a blink.'

Shaggy-coat had had only seconds then to steady the aim, tighten his grip, take up the pressure and blaze at a point-blank target. But he had wasted at least three in another grin of satisfaction and flick of his gaze to the woman, then back to Jonas, seconds in which he might have been aware of the gleam of Jonas's Colt clearing leather, when he might have lost his concentration in staring at the barrel, cursed that he had not ordered the man to drop his gun-belt, and known in the suddenly blinding flash, the shattering roar that he had left it too late, been too slow against a lightning draw.

The shaggy-haired coat was already darkening under the stain of free-flowing blood as Jonas watched its wearer crumple like a heap of dead fur, then dropped instantly to one knee with Duckback and his half-drawn gun at a ragged holster clear in his aim.

The second flash and roar seemed to scythe at the very light, dropping Duckback with his fingers still not curled to a cold butt and his hooded eye flickering crazily.

He hit the dirt with a thud, the echo of the shot and snorting of horses ringing in his ears.

Jonas spun like a whipped top to Alicia, but too late to catch her as her eyes rolled, her mouth opened on a gasp and she passed out.

Alicia Furneaux stirred with the sun hot and glaring on her face, a trickle of sweat slipping like warm grease down her neck, and a throat that seemed to be coated with gravel.

She groaned, wiped a hand across her brow and struggled to sit upright against a smooth shelving of rock.

It was a long half-minute then before her eyes were fully open and focusing first on Jonas where he squatted tending the coffee pot at the still smoking fire, and then, in a slow fearful turn of her gaze, to the dead bodies, the smears and stains of dark blood.

She stifled a shiver, sniffed on the lingering smell of cordite and death and made a croaking attempt to clear her gravel-bed throat.

'Any chance—' she began.

'Fresh coffee comin' up in two minutes,' clipped Jonas, his back to Alicia. 'And then you've got ten exactly to drink it and be ready to shift.'

Alicia's lips tightened dramatically. 'Don't you think you might just spare the time to ask how I am?' she croaked again, almost choking on the words. 'And wouldn't it be decent to explain this. . . these bodies, the blood, the killing?'

'Can see how yuh are, ma'am,' said Jonas into the smoke. 'Been lookin' to yuh for close on a half-hour. You'll live.'

'Well, I'm genuinely reassured to hear that!' mocked Alicia. 'Pity you can't be as positive about the men lying there.' She swallowed and wiped a hand over her sweating face, smudging grey dirt into her cheeks. 'Did you have to kill them, Mr Jonas?'

Smoke curled in a sudden pothering. 'Yes, ma'am,' grunted Jonas, easing the coffee pot from the fire. 'I did too. That, or get m'self killed and leave you to a couple of animals. Didn't seem to be much of an option to me.' He poured steaming coffee into a tin mug, came upright and crossed to the rock shelving. 'It trouble you?' he asked, offering the mug.

Alicia Furneaux's lips tightened again as she tossed her hair regally into her neck and spread her arms across the rock. 'Mr Jonas,' she began, her eyes suddenly wide and gleaming, 'I may not be your idea of an all-weathers, bush and scrub mountain trail girl – I most definitely am not – but I do know and have standards, and killing men, whoever they are, whatever they are, in such a cold-blooded, determined manner, is something I find disturbing.

'And you seem to kill with such ease. Why? And just what sort of a life have you been leading – are leading – to use a gun in the way you do? I appreciate our difficulties, the dangers we have faced and still have facing us, and am grateful for everything you have done, but to continue—'

'Ten minutes,' snapped Jonas, thrusting the tin mug at the woman. 'And in case you ain't noticed, we've gotten you a horse, courtesy of the vermin here, so we're trailin' hard and fast for Riverbend. Ain't sure if we'll make it, but I'm sure as hell bothered about tryin'. Now shift yuh butt, lady, and let's quit the whimperin' over dead bodies.' He shielded his eyes as he gazed into the high blue sky. 'Buzzards ain't complainin'!'

NINE

Silence – a part of it welcome, a part too eerie and a touch too deep for comfort. Jonas hummed quietly to himself for a moment as he encouraged his mount over the rough, sun-baked track, listened for the clip of the woman's horse behind him and contemplated his next move on the trail to Riverbend.

The humming faded and he grunted on a note of aggravation. Damn the woman, he reflected, maybe she was right, maybe he did kill easy, no questions asked, no explanations expected.

But, then, miss sassy, classy Alicia Furneaux had been cosseted in the comforts of St Louis since birth; not for her the home shack in the mountains, a down-and-out pa and a ma who had died struggling to feed her child. Not for her the ragbag, hand-to-mouth years when you scraped a leftover living and survived by the code: kill or be killed. The gun was law and you stood to it. Or died by it.

Jonas murmured absently to his thoughts, blinked on the shimmering glare and shielded his eyes as he scanned the surrounding mountains and sharper, higher peaks. All quiet. Silence.

Nothing save the clip of hoofs, the gentle tinkle of the relaxed tack. Not so much as the drifting hawk.

And still the woman stayed silent, as she had since leaving the fire and the bodies of the dead drifters. Two bits to a tin mug you could almost pick the anger and disgust from her eyes, he thought behind a slow grin. So be it, if that was what it was going to take to reach Riverbend.

'Shall we be there by nightfall, Mr Jonas?' called Alicia, with a toss of her hair and a subdued sigh against the clamouring heat.

'That's the plan of it, ma'am,' he answered calmly, the aggravation bitten back, the reflections broken. 'First light tomorrow is the latest. My reckonin' puts the *Ada Benson* at Riverbend by mid afternoon. She don't stop, but eases her speed some for the slow water loop. That's goin' to be our chance.'

Alicia resumed her silence for a moment, then, as she swatted at a pestering fly, said, 'I'm sure you're right, Mr Jonas, but how are we supposed to attract the attention of the boat and, perhaps more to the point, how are we going to get aboard it? Although I'm sure you've given that some thought too.' There was no mistaking the sarcastic quip in her voice.

Jonas preoccupied himself with scanning the peaks before he answered. 'No, ma'am, can't say I have. Riverbend don't exactly inspire with what it's got on offer. Old trapper's shack and that's about the sum of it.'

'So we're going to have to trust to luck?' The sarcasm had a keener edge. 'Trust, I suppose, that

the Cheyenne have somehow lost their way,
Birdboy remained in Cripple Creek, and we, by
some miracle, have a means of boarding the *Ada
Benson* by any "luck" that happens our way.
Highly unlikely, I'd have thought.'

'You'd be right there, lady,' said Jonas lightly.
'Too damned right.' He could picture the indigna-
tion creasing her face. 'But it ain't goin' to happen
like that. Not no how it ain't. Fact is, Eagle Neck's
bucks won't be that far behind us even now, and
there's been one of Birdboy's sidekicks trailin'
them higher reaches there for the past half-hour.
He ain't there for his health.'

Alicia's glance into the mountain slopes and
bluffs was tight and worried, raising a new beading of sweat across her brow. 'Are you sure? I don't
see anything,' she said, the tone softer, the
sarcasm forgotten.

'Oh, yes, ma'am, I'm sure, but he's mebbe no
threat right now. My guess is he'll track us 'til he's
sure just where we're headin', then pull away,
report back to Birdboy.'

'And you're going to let him?'

'Well, ma'am,' said Jonas, slowing his mount
until the woman drew level, 'there ain't exactly a
lot I can do about it, is there? Chances are he'd
give me the slip and be long gone before I got a
hundred feet into them reaches. Could try killin'
him on a long shot with the Winchester we helped
ourselves to from Shaggy-coat back there, but,
like yuh say, there's mebbe been enough killin'.'

'That's unworthy of you, Mr Jonas,' flared
Alicia, her eyes glinting. 'You know perfectly well
what I meant, and as for. . . . Oh, it doesn't matter.

Let's just get on with this as fast as we can.' She cracked the reins through her fingers.

Jonas grinned wryly as he pulled at the brim of his hat, then delved into his shirt pocket for a cheroot, lit it and blew a line of smoke into the glare. But his eyes were narrowed and his gaze intense as he scanned the mountains again.

The lone rider was still with them, still watching.

He would stay always just those few yards out of gunshot range, thought Jonas an hour later, as he guided Alicia Furneaux into the first of the long drift from the high country back to the Big Muddy.

He would be content to watch, track, move at whatever pace Jonas set, and move off just as quietly when the time came.

But the rider himself and his presence was not at the real heart of Jonas's concern.

It was the fact that the loss of the woman from the cabin and her disappearance into the mountains had been acted on so quickly. Birdboy and whoever the sidekicks he had working with him in Cripple Creek had reacted speedily and thoroughly, picking up Jonas's trail almost as quickly as Eagle Neck's scouting party. It was only a matter of time before either or both of them caught up again, Birdboy being more than aware of the *Ada Benson's* schedule and Eagle Neck impatient for his prize and retribution for the loss of his bucks.

Jonas swallowed, cleared the sweat at his neck and turned to the woman. 'We're movin' down to the pines, ma'am. Should have the river in sight in about an hour. We'll be on the track to Riverbend by dusk.'

'The rider is still following?' asked Alicia.

'Oh, yes, ma'am, he's still there. He ain't through yet.'

'Will he keep following?'

'For a while, 'til he figures he's seen enough.'

Alicia bit on her lower lip. 'Shouldn't we. . . I mean supposing. . . . I'm not sure quite what I mean, but it just doesn't seem much to our advantage to let the man see all he wants and relay the information back to Birdboy unchallenged.'

'Nor is it, ma'am, but like I've said—'

'I've heard what you've said, Mr Jonas. You've made your opinions perfectly clear. I'm just wondering. . . .' She tightened her grip on the reins and tossed her hair into her neck. 'Well, it's perhaps not very sensible – in fact, I'm sure it's not – but if we were to split up—'

'Split up?' choked Jonas.

'Not permanently, you understand,' said Alicia, hurriedly. 'No, nothing like that. I mean split up just long enough to make the rider out there wonder just what on earth we're doing and curious enough to. . . .' She tossed her hair again. 'Well, I don't know, but I'm sure you would, Mr Jonas. At least that way we might delay Birdboy by a few hours.'

'But, ma'am,' reasoned Jonas, 'if we were to do as you say, that scumbag out there would be Colt-to-a-holster certain to come for you.'

'Precisely,' quipped Alicia. 'That would be the whole idea.'

'But you'd be offerin' yourself as a lure, a bait – and you've made your feelin's clear enough over that.'

'The Cheyenne were different,' said Alicia, staring ahead. 'What I did there – what you made me do – was degrading.'

'Well, I'm sure as hell sorry about that!' flared Jonas. 'Fact that we're both alive don't mean a spit, I suppose?'

'This is no time for arguing, Mr Jonas,' said Alicia, reining her mount to a halt at Jonas's side. 'The pines are ahead and we're in full view of the tracking rider. Here is the perfect place to appear to split up. You go one way, I go the other. So, do we do it and buy ourselves a little more time from the attentions of Birdboy, or do we carry on as we are and keep our fingers crossed that we get incredibly lucky? The choice is yours.'

TEN

It was crazy and a risk that was about as precarious as a boulder rocking on the brink of a precipice, but it might just work, damn it. And if it did, they would have a new edge over Birdboy that would take some making up. In fact, thought Jonas, trailing alone into the pines, they might make it on a clear run to Riverbend and be aboard the *Ada Benson* before Birdboy realized it.

He trailed deeper until he was in the thickest of the tree cover, reined up, patted his mount's neck and eased back in the saddle to watch, listen and wait.

Alicia Furneaux had continued along the narrow track where it twisted away from the rocky slopes and outcrops back to the scrub and steadily thickening pine growth. She had glanced at Jonas only once before passing into the shadows, a glance that had been as much a look of fearful hope that this was going to work as it had of how and when.

She had not looked back, seen nothing of the lone rider's sudden halt, the few minutes of hesitation and indecision as he debated whether to report back to Birdboy, keep watching, or follow the woman. He must have pondered on why the pair had split at this point, where the woman would be heading and where, if anywhere, her escort might be trailing. Or would he be lurking?

The rider broke from the bluff in a flurry of snapping reins and clattering hoofs, his gaze already set and narrowed on the pines for a sight of Alicia, his face gleaming under a lathering of sweat. This move had not been planned. He had not figured for it, but he guessed Birdboy would approve.

Jonas watched as horse and rider approached. He would let them pass just far enough down the track for the man to catch the briefest glimpse of Alicia who would be moving as slowly as might seem natural and as her nerve would allow.

The rider slowed, the reins short and tight in his hands, his body tensed, eyes shifting like an animal's to the left, to the right, ahead, a quick glance to the back of him.

Pause, wait, listen. There was the snap of a twig up front, a hoof cracking through tinder-dry scrub, a scuff of thicker growth, snort of a horse, Alicia's murmured words of encouragement.

Jonas swallowed, his mind reeling on the image of the woman, watchful and stifling a shudder as her eyes probed every thicket of shadow, every shape that would seem then to be something more than it was – an arm, a leg, a staring face, a body that was simply there.

The rider was moving, sure now of where the woman was, how far ahead, but beginning to wonder again about her escort. His gaze sharpened as if to look around the pines, under the tangles of scrub, the sweat thickening across his face, hanging like bright beads on his stubble.

Jonas slid carefully from his mount, patting its neck as his feet found the ground and he hitched the reins across a limb of bough. He waited, catching the almost whispered tinkle of the rider's tack, the ghostly tread of hoofs.

Had Alicia halted, frozen in her fear, regretting she had so much as thought of this crazy scheme let alone gone ahead with it, or was she simply calculating the odds of Jonas being right there in the steps of the rider?

'Hold it right there, lady.'

The voice grated from the rider's throat like a thickset cough, a Colt already levelled in his hand.

'I ain't for harmin' yuh, but you'd sure as hell better come quiet. We're in a hurry and I ain't for messin'.'

The man hawked and spat, his mount's steps towards Alicia scuffing heavily through pine needles and scrub.

Jonas had edged as close now as he dared, almost on to the track Alicia and the rider had followed, the man's back a dark blur in the tangle of branches and thrusting brush.

'Who are you? What do you want?' croaked Alicia, from somewhere in the shadowy depths of the trees.

'Yuh ain't for havin' me spell that out for yuh?' sneered the man. 'Hell, you've been givin' us the run-around for long enough, ever since that scumbag drifter took yuh from the cabin. And just where did he disappear to?' The man half-turned, first left, then right, forcing Jonas to crouch low against the shafting light.

'He's gone down to the river,' said Alicia quickly, a touch of panic in her voice. 'Check things out.'

The man grunted. 'So you keep movin', lady. We got ground to cover before nightfall.'

Alicia stepped her mount carefully closer, parting the brush and branches tentatively. 'Where are you taking me?' she said, her voice cracking. 'I have a right to know.'

'Zackman and Birdboy are waitin' on you – and their patience is wearin' awful thin.' The man spat and gestured with the Colt. 'So let's move it, eh?'

'Zackman?' said Alicia, easing the horse a step closer. 'Who is Zackman? I've never heard of him.'

'You'll be hearin' plenty of him, lady,' grinned the man. 'You bet! If you thought Birdboy was a bit coarse for your taste, you ain't seen nothin' yet.'

Alicia shivered but still managed to toss her hair defiantly.

Jonas's eyes had narrowed, his mind racing on the name Zackman. Arno Zackman, he thought, with a lick of his lips, sure he had heard of him; a smooth, double-dealing gunslinger out of Fort Bragg and Montana territory. Not a name to be welcomed at any table, especially when the stakes were as high as a shipment of gold. Zackman would be playing it as rough as was needed.

'Are we heading for Cripple Creek?' persisted Alicia, determined to extract all the information she could. 'Because if that's where you intend taking me, Mr. . . . I'm sorry, I didn't catch your name.'

'Didn't give it, t'ain't necessary,' scowled the man. 'Now, you just get movin'. And no, since yuh ask, we ain't headin' for Cripple Creek. We got a rendezvous with Zackman, Birdboy and the others at a place called Riverbend, up-river from here and I plan to be there by sundown. So shift!'

Jonas swallowed, winced and licked at cold sweat, at the same time hissing a long curse on a still longer sigh. Riverbend! Hell!

Alicia had managed to stifle and swallow a choking gasp and bring her gaze hurriedly into focus on the man's face. 'I have never heard of the place,' she huffed as haughtily as she could summon. 'What is it – apart from being undesirable?'

A frown furrowed Alicia's brow as she tossed her hair again and tried desperately to look beyond the man, over his shoulder into the scrub and shadows for a sight of Jonas.

'Riverbend ain't no place particular, and it ain't goin' to be a spit of use to you knowin', anyhow,' said the man, his impatience growing, the Colt probing, hovering. 'Now I ain't goin' to tell yuh one more time, lady, you move, or I get to shiftin' you personally, and you wouldn't want that. Understand?'

Alicia hesitated, uncertain of what to do, where to turn; whether to be defiant or relent to the man's demands.

She stared at the levelled Colt. 'Guns do not concern me, whoever-you-are, and you would not dare use it,' she sneered, her body stiffening as she sat the saddle to her full height. 'I am far too valuable alive.'

She risked another glance over the man's shoulder, but this time his steady gaze had followed her eyes, and he swung himself and horse round instantly, the Colt already blazing at a shape that had not been there before.

ELEVEN

A scream, like the screech of a startled bird, broke deep in Alicia's throat. Horses whinnied, bucked and snorted. The man growled behind the spitting roar of his Colt, realizing in the clearing smoke, the haze of cordite, that the shape he had seen a moment ago was no longer there, had somehow shrunk back to the scrub, melted on the light, or been no more than the shadow of a ghost.

'Sonofa-goddam-bitch!' he cursed, spinning round to the woman again, only to see her backing slowly, defiantly into the trees, the reins of her mount tight in her hand.

'Damn you,' spat the man, the sweat flying from his face, his eyes wide and gleaming in his rage and the creeping suffocation of a trap closing on him. 'You stay right where you are, bitch. One more step—'

A twig cracked and snapped like a shot behind him. The man spun round again, slipping like a snake from the saddle, his Colt stiff, levelled but silent as he saw something move, a shadow grow, drift and disappear as if swallowed on the shafting light.

'Hell!' The man sank to a crouch, blinked on his sweat and peered disbelievingly at the tangle of trees where now there was only a blanket of darkness, but nothing of Alicia or her horse.

'Seems like it just ain't goin' to be your day, don't it?' said the voice from somewhere deep within the thickening gloom of trees and scrub. 'Know just how yuh feel. . . .'

The man sank lower into the crouch, the Colt levelled like a gleaming claw on a probing antennae. 'Who the hell are you, mister?' he croaked. 'You the fella from back there at the cabin?'

'Well,' drawled Jonas casually, 'I guess you might say I happened by the place, and I ain't personally one for seein' no lady bein' mistreated by scumbag vermin the likes of the sort I found there.'

The man growled and lunged in the same moment, the Colt blazing wildly, lead flying without aim or target as rage, frustration, fear bubbled, merged and exploded in his stumbling burst for the trees.

He had taken four, five, a half-dozen steps, the gun still emptying, when the Winchester retorted with a crash of rapid fire that seemed to drown the Colt and fill the trees with echoes that hung from their tops.

The man was down, flat on his face, bleeding but dead in seconds, and the silence drifting in again when Jonas stepped from the shadows, the rifle easy in his grip, shielded his eyes against the fading sun's glare and began to reckon how long it would take on a fast, direct route to the banks of the Big Muddy.

It was some while, before Alicia could find the stomach to join him at the side of the stiffening body.

'Simple enough,' said Jonas, ducking and weaving carefully through the lowslung boughs of the tight-packed pines as he led the mounts on foot towards the river, 'the rat we left back there said all we needed to know. And that's thanks to you, ma'am. Yuh did a good job.'

Alicia followed thoughtfully in Jonas's steps, her gaze drifting between being alert and watchful for what might be lurking in the trees, to blank introspection.

'Ma'am?' said Jonas, a frown deepening above his stare.

'Sorry,' fluttered Alicia, running a hand through her hair, 'I was. . . somewhere else. It doesn't matter. You were saying?'

'About what yuh did back there. We learned a lot. Save ourselves a whole heap of trouble and mebbe our lives by avoidin' Riverbend. Lord above knows how Arno Zackman got himself tied into this but, believe me, he's trouble. Crossed him before, and I ain't for renewin' his acquaintance 'til I'm forced.'

'So we're heading for Cripple Creek?' said Alicia.

'No, ma'am, that we surely ain't. Can't take the chance on Eagle Neck sittin' tight. He'll be wantin' our scalps, and makin' real certain we don't get within a spit of the Creek.'

'Birdboy and this man, Zackman, at Riverbend,

the Cheyenne barring our way into Cripple Creek. . . . Do we have any options left, Mr Jonas?'

'Only one.'

'That being?'

'We cross the river, ma'am.'

'Cross it?' frowned Alicia. 'But how on earth do we do that? And don't say swim, because I can't.'

'No swimmin' involved, ma'am – leastways, I hope not – but we might make it in a canoe.'

Alicia ducked a low branch, tossed her hair and faced Jonas where he had halted in the deepening gloom and waited for her to catch up. 'Yes,' she said with a hint of condenscension, 'we might very well make it across the Big Muddy in a canoe – if, of course, we had a canoe, which, let me remind you, we do not.' She slung her weight to one hip and flattened her hands at her waist. 'So? she asked with a lift of her eyebrows.

'True enough, ma'am,' mused Jonas, nuzzling his mount's nose, 'but I reckon I know where we very well might find a canoe.'

Alicia continued to stare, the eyebrows still raised.

'Old trapper by the name of Neilson used to operate hereabouts, this side of Riverbend and north of Cripple Creek. He'd sometimes winter at the Creek, but always leave his canoe up-river for fear of being tempted to wager it in one of his hell-fire gambling bouts. And believe me, ma'am, they were just that, hell on fire, sometimes lastin' for days. Old Neilson would have wagered the clothes off his grandma's back, and probably did, if he figured he was cradlin' a winnin' hand!'

Jonas smiled softly to himself and shook his

head. 'Poor devil passed on peaceful enough last
fall. Died playin' poker in O'Shea's bar. . . .
Anyhow, I don't reckon they ever found that canoe
when they came to figurin' the old man's personal
possessions, so mebbe it's still right there in a
cave on the banks of the Big Muddy at Cooper's
Drift.'

'He told you where he'd hidden it?' frowned
Alicia.

'Came down river with him one fall. Was with
him when he stashed it.'

'Which is not to say he continued to use the
same cave, or hid the canoe there last year.'

'You're right there, ma'am. Chance we're goin'
to have to take.'

Alicia relaxed and tossed her hair. 'Another no-
choice situation, Mr Jonas.'

'Just so. You're learnin' fast, ma'am!'

'And I don't have much choice in that either, do
I?' said Alicia. 'Lead on!'

Once mounted and on to the clear track heading
for the river, the pace quickened and the progress
remained unhindered. Jonas figured for making it
to the Drift well before nightfall. And they would
need to if they were going to have a hope of find-
ing the canoe.

Jonas grunted quietly to his thoughts as he
watched for the turns and twists of the track,
ducked the threatening reach of pine boughs and
marauding branches and listened to the steady
scuff of hoofs through scrub and jangle of tack on
the following mount.

Alicia Furneaux was holding up well, he mused, a whole sight better in fact than he would have reckoned.

He grunted again. Hell, given a fair share of any luck going, they might yet make it to the *Ada Benson*. Only problem right now being the need for that canoe.

His thoughts began to spin as the twilight deepened, the first chill of the day setting his sweat tingling, the shadows lunging like blind warriors.

Where were Eagle Neck's bucks now, he wondered; how far behind? Birdboy and Zackman had figured it right in making for Riverbend, but what were their plans from there on? Supposing they too became intent on boarding the *Ada Benson*. Could it be done? And where, damn it, would that leave the price on Alicia Furneaux's head?

Jonas had a sudden black vision of bodies floating in the swirling waters of the Big Muddy, faces he recognized. . . .

'Is that the river I can hear up ahead, Mr Jonas?' called Alicia at his back.

TWELVE

The tumbling roar of the Big Muddy fell across the silence of the night like a warning to stay clear. Alicia shivered, as if having heard it, and pulled nervously at the skimpy protection of the ill-fitting shirt and worn pants against the damp chill. She peered intently into the darkness for a sight of the flow.

'Not a deal to see, ma'am,' said Jonas, the reins soft in his hands. 'Sound tells yuh all you need to know.' He pointed to his right. 'We dismount and lead the horses along this track to where it drops away to an inlet. That's where we'll find the caves. Any amount of 'em hereabouts.'

'But you know the one? You can find it?' hissed Alicia, as if afraid the river might be listening.

'Hope so,' said Jonas, slipping from the saddle. 'Soon goin' to find out, aren't we?'

Alicia shivered again, pulled at the shirt and glanced quickly at Jonas. She thought better of saying anything.

The track dropping to the softer shoreline of the inlet was narrow, tight and shelving steeply –

tricky to negotiate in full daylight; a nightmare in the dark.

Jonas led, whispering and murmuring softly to his mount as he encouraged its tentative footfalls, paused for the confidence to grow, checked on Alicia's progress, and moved on again.

They were close into a full hour of cold, clinging sweats, curses stifled under anxious breath, slips and slides before they finally reached the soft sand and scree of packed stone.

'Welcome to Cooper's Drift, ma'am,' announced Jonas. 'Such as it is and what you can see of it. Caves are back there. We'll hitch the mounts and go take a look.'

'When we've found the canoe – *if* we find the canoe – when do we cross?' asked Alicia, wiping the cold sweat from her face.

'A half-hour before first light. First hint of it in the east, but ahead of it comin' up full. Plenty of shadows then, ma'am, and if the wind's in the right quarter and the surface as smooth as it ever gets at the Drift, we might get lucky and be across there and headin' for Riverbend in. . . . Yeah, well, we'll have to see.'

Alicia nodded. 'Is time running out for us, Mr Jonas? How long have we got? Wouldn't it be to our advantage to cross as soon as we find the canoe?'

'Too dangerous, ma'am. You can hear that flow out there. It's tellin' you plenty if you listen close. One false move, get yourself in the wrong run of the current, holed on rocks, snagged on root or driftwood, and—' Jonas gestured wildly, 'you're scuppered and gone before you can take your last breath.'

'I see,' said Alicia with a toss of her hair. 'Well, I'm trusting to you, Mr Jonas. You seem to know best.'

'No, ma'am, not best necessarily. Just that I get to prayin' real hard.'

Once again, Alicia thought better of saying anything.

They were another hour after hitching the mounts before the first of the web of caves had been investigated. 'Just don't look the same in the dark,' Jonas had complained, leading Alicia in the scrambling, skin-grazing exploration over rocks, boulders and razor-edged stones.

But they pressed on, Jonas standing back occasionally to scan what he could make out of the rock face and the darker spreads of the mouths of caves, his hurriedly constructed and lucifer-lit brushwood torch lighting the way.

'It's gotta be here, damnit,' he grunted, pausing for a moment, the first hint of anxiety in his voice.

Alicia rubbed her eyes, blinked, hugged herself against the chill night air and narrowed her gaze. 'There are more caves there,' she said, pointing to a seemingly blank sprawl of rocks. 'Beyond those boulders.'

'Hell, old Neilson would've had some job humpin' his canoe that distance over boulders that big.'

'Perhaps that was the whole idea – he was making it difficult for the craft to be found.'

'Could be, ma'am,' acknowledged Jonas, lifting the torch higher. 'I was pretty sure he used a cave back here, but could be he got canny in his old age.'

'Only one way to find out, Mr Jonas,' smiled Alicia.

It was in the second cave they entered that they found it, beached like some stranded whale beneath a dank, holed blanket.

Jonas handed the torch to Alicia and pulled the covering aside with a flourish. 'There it is, ma'am: Pop Neilson's "flying fish" as he called it, complete with paddles. As river-worthy as it ever was.' He stepped closer and rubbed the craft's side affectionately. 'Seen some miles, ma'am, and some wild days markin' every one of 'em. Could tell a fair tale.'

He grunted, stared in silence for a moment, then turned sharply to Alicia. 'Best get yourself a couple of hours' rest, ma'am, while we got the chance. I'll go collect the bedrolls and anythin' else useful we can carry from the mounts, then turn 'em loose. They'll make their way down-river to the Creek, but not before we're long gone.'

Alicia nodded and shivered. 'What are our chances now, Mr Jonas?' she asked.

Jonas waited a moment, his gaze tight on the woman's face, a face that had changed a good deal since he had first seen it at the cabin; dirt-smudged, weathered, tense but wary, and right now creased with tiredness. How many in St Louis would recognize her tonight, he wondered? How many would want to?

'Well, ma'am, we've found the canoe, and that's gotta be a bonus,' he said quietly. 'It don't mean we're home and dry to Riverbend, but once we cross that river, yeah, you could say we got a fair chance.'

Alicia half-smiled in the spasm of a shiver.

'There ain't no sayin' as to Eagle Neck's thinkin',' Jonas continued. 'Cheyenne go their own way and there's no how you can change that. Mebbe they'll back off, mebbe they won't. Me – I'd say they won't, leastways not quite yet. Birdboy and Zackman, on the other hand, ain't no way for givin' up, and certainly not while you're still on the loose, ma'am, and your pa and the gold dust aboard the *Ada Benson* – which is why we gotta be there at Riverbend when the steamer comes through.'

Alicia nodded again as her eyelids fluttered in her tiredness. 'So like I say, ma'am. . . .'

But that was as far as Jonas went. In the next moment he had taken the torch from Alicia's grip, doused it and guided her gently in his arms to the back of the cave.

Midnight had come and gone, Jonas had turned the mounts loose to the track, put the bedroll blankets to good use over the sleeping woman, stashed the saddles and brought the canoe to the mouth of the cave, when the sweat in his neck changed from hot and sticky to cold and stinging.

The shadows – very definitely in the shapes of men — had drifted across his line of vision softly, silently and without pausing, but Jonas had made no attempt to move from where he was seated on rocks only yards from the canoe.

He swallowed, shrugged his shoulders beneath the draped blanket, and lowered his head as if dozing, at the same time sharpening his gaze to watch for the next movement. It came within seconds. Another flitting, scurrying slip of shadows between the rocks at the line between the Big Muddy's tumbling rush and the riverbank.

Two Cheyenne bucks, tracking fast from where a larger party had discovered their dead companions; keeping their distance, no intention of attacking; there simply to watch till close on sunup and then report back to Eagle Neck.

Jonas shrugged again, his gaze tight and steady. The Cheyenne had tracked at speed; determined, no compromise, no plan to pull away. They were staying with the hunt. They were beginning to hate.

A whole sight more to the point they must have seen the canoe. The Cheyenne would know precisely what Jonas had in mind.

But did he still have an edge? Only one – if he had the nerve to play it.

He settled. He would wait, stay watchful and be ready to move the instant the Cheyenne tracked away. Another hour, two at most.

Exactly two had elapsed when the shadows crossed through the faint moonlight and disappeared into the darkness downriver.

Jonas remained in the rocks for some long minutes until he was quite certain the bucks had not doubled back or simply shifted position. He watched, waited, breathed easy, began to fathom

how quickly the canoe could be moved to the flow.
And when to wake the banker's daughter.

THIRTEEN

She stirred to the softest touch, her eyes opening instantly, as wide and round as milky moons. Jonas put a finger to his lips for quiet. 'We've had company, ma'am,' he whispered. 'Cheyenne bucks. They're gone now, but they'll be back. They know we're here and they've seen the canoe, so we're goin' to have to move.'

'But it's still dark,' murmured Alicia, propping herself on one elbow. 'We can't cross 'til it's light, can we?'

'Goin' to have to give it our best, ma'am. We hang about here waitin' for sun-up and the Cheyenne'll be down our throats like flies.'

'In that case—' Alicia winced at the jarring aches in the sudden movement. 'In that case,' she began again with a toss of her hair and straightening of the shirt, 'we must go.' She scrambled to her feet in an ungainly twist of limbs. 'Thank you for letting me sleep, Mr Jonas. I needed the rest. But what about you? Have you slept?'

'No, ma'am, can't say I have. But I get used to it. Goes with the way of life.' Jonas's grin faltered a touch in the thought of his plans for clean sheets and a proper bed in Cripple Creek.

'You should settle down,' smiled Alicia, scrambling her hair into a roughly tied ponytail.

'Yes, ma'am,' said Jonas, turning to narrow his gaze on the darkness beyond the cave, 'I'll give it some thought – assumin' I get the chance.'

The Winchester, one blanket, a canteen of water, pack of jerky beef – 'And that's it, ma'am,' Jonas announced as he slid the few belongings into the canoe. 'Nothin' more. We need to stay light to move at speed. And speed is all we're thinkin' about.'

'I've never done this before,' said Alicia, eyeing the canoe suspiciously where it rocked gently in the quieter flow at the riverbank.

'No, ma'am, don't suppose yuh have,' answered Jonas, watchful of the rocks and the shadows behind them. 'Don't let it bother yuh. I'll call the orders – to paddle left or right – and you follow my pace, do as I say. And don't look back. Just keep the other bank in sight and head for it.'

'The river looks quiet enough here.'

'Might look it, but don't be fooled none. Big Muddy's about as fickle as a snappy woman in the rainy season – no offence intended. She's got more dangers out there than I've had. . . . Yeah, well, that don't matter none. We just stay wide awake.'

'And pray, I suppose,' added Alicia flatly.

'Yes, ma'am, we do plenty of that.'

Minutes later, the Big Muddy's roar had welcomed the canoe to its swirling waters.

They moved swiftly but stealthily, Jonas taking no chances, opting for quieter water wherever he could find it, keeping the canoe's bows headed in only one direction. There was still nothing like a gathering of daylight; only the now fitful and waning moon's glow, the bruising night clouds and the faintest chinks to a dawn in the far eastern skies.

Jonas worked his paddle at a steady pace, conscious of the demands on Alicia to work to her own with one eye on the rate he was setting. She said nothing, the only sound of her being the lift and fall of her breathing in the effort.

The course was simple enough: diagonally north, against the flow, for as far as their strength would take them or until their luck ran out. Jonas reckoned a landing almost anywhere on the opposite bank following this course would bring them within a few short miles of the Riverbend loop and the river's meander. From there to getting Alicia Furneaux aboard the *Ada Benson* would be. . . . He was pushing an already frail slice of luck there, he thought, bending his back to the paddle as the flow strengthened suddenly and they slid like a twist of flotsam into the teeth of a bite of rocks.

'Rough water, ma'am,' called Jonas over his shoulder. 'Just hold her steady. Be through it in no time.'

He was hopeful, maybe sounding a mite too optimistic when he took a closer look at the raw, jagged line of exposed rocks and the river tumbling like a flood between them.

Spray flew in a misted shower, soaking clothes, skin, hair, stinging deep into Jonas's eyes until he was forced to squint for the next looming bulk of rock and plunge the paddle to avoid it.

Alicia cried out in the icy chill of the sudden soaking, croaked inaudible words and blinked on what seemed to have become a heaving cauldron of flying spray and threshing water.

'Keep her steady, ma'am!' shouted Jonas, above the hiss and trembling roar, his arms and body jolted as the canoe thudded into and scraped along a grazing of razored rocks, the whole structure threatening to split like an overipe seed pod.

The canoe raced on, channelled now between rocks, at the mercy of the flow and beginning to yaw to the current.

'We're going downriver, Mr Jonas,' yelled Alicia, her face glistening with sweat and spray. 'I was under the impression—'

'I know, ma'am, I know.'

Jonas thrust the paddle against a rock, pushed the canoe clear, plunged the paddle and worked as if in a crazed frenzy to propel the craft to where he could see the gentle swirl of calmer waters.

'Paddle like hell, ma'am,' he called. 'Keep to my stroke. We've got a break comin' up.'

They worked on frenetically, their muscles numbing to the pain of effort, their eyes smarting as the spray lifted through steadily brightening light, the shadows seeming to circle them like hovering crows.

Jonas plunged the paddle again and boosted the rate, felt the thrust behind him as Alicia followed suit, heard her groan, winced and was almost tempted to slump as the canoe broke from the white water race and slipped softly into the calmer flow.

'Ease up, ma'am,' he ordered. 'I'll take her on. We can hold to this run now for a while.'

He half turned to catch the briefest glimpse of Alicia, her arms like broken vines at her sides, her head hanging to her knees. Jonas grunted and pushed on, the canoe gliding to the merest whisper of movement.

The morning was coming up on a freshening breeze, but the thickening clouds to the north already had him worried.

'Is that bad weather coming up, Mr Jonas?' called Alicia, on another swish of her paddle to the steady rhythm through the easy running flow.

'You got it, ma'am,' said Jonas, unable to swallow the gloom in his voice.

'Perhaps we should get ashore 'til it passes.'

'No sayin' as to how long it might last. Could be hours, and we ain't got the time. We keep goin'.'

Alicia was silent for a moment. 'How far now?' she finally called again.

'Some miles yet, ma'am. Another couple of hours if the water stays calm.'

Jonas glanced round him. All quiet and as it should be on the banks where the breeze had cleared the early mist but left a brooding darkness under the heavy skies. The higher peaks were still shrouded, the rocky slopes as grey as funeral faces.

His gaze narrowed on the flow ahead. Sheer rock faces coming up on the left; the river sweeping slowly to a bend; heavy pine growth, scrub and a low shoreline to the right. He would bring the canoe into the lee of the rock face, hug the deeper water and maximum shadow. Once into the bend and on course to the freer flow—

'Mr Jonas!'

He half-turned again at the grating panic in Alicia's voice.

'Look.' She pointed a shaking hand to the pine-covered bank and the inlet break where two canoes were nosing into the flow like hungry sharks. 'Cheyenne!' she shuddered.

The sweat in Jonas's neck began to bite and prickle as he tightened his grip on the already flashing paddle.

FOURTEEN

The bows of the canoe scythed into the deeper water like a honed blade. Jonas gasped in the effort, eased the pace and glanced quickly at Alicia, her head thrown back, sweat dripping from her face, eyes closed in the darkness of despair and effort.

'We gotta keep goin', ma'am,' swallowed Jonas on a cracking throat. 'Them Cheyenne are comin' at some speed.'

Alicia's eyes sprung open. 'We can't outrun them, can we?' she croaked.

'Goin' to give it one helluva try!'

'How did they catch up so quickly? I thought—'

'Trackin' Cheyenne are like your own shadow, ma'am: always right there on your heels. Don't never go away.' He glanced over Alicia's shoulder. 'Here they come, damn it! Let's shift. Bend your back for your life, ma'am!'

The canoe shot forward again, this time seeming to leap for a moment as Jonas picked up the pace and momentum. The flow swirled but deepened, giving their paddles the leverage for speed. Jonas grunted, winced on the stabbing pains in his shoulders and wondered just how well constructed and cared for old Pop Neilson's 'flying fish' really was. He had trusted the canoe with his life, so maybe it had an inbuilt feel for survival. God willing!

The paddles continued to flash, the surface cut to white water as Jonas paced on, feeling the thrust of Alicia's effort at his back, hearing her grunts to the rhythmic lift and fall, scythe and swish.

The Cheyenne's canoes had been built for the Big Muddy. They would be sleek, fast, designed for the lightning raid on some foundering keelboat, the bucks aboard them young and strong, the cream of Eagle Neck's band of followers.

It might be only a matter of time before they broke their course to a pincer attack, one canoe to the left, one to the right, closing and then narrowing the channel of escape until Jonas and the woman had nowhere to go, no water left and would be forced to the bank.

Alicia gasped and shuddered, in one moment chilled under the lathering of sweat that had soaked her clothes to sodden rags, in the next her skin boiling and bubbling under the heat of strain, her eyes unable to focus, mouth open, every pore of her body oozing sweat, every muscle stretched and tensed to limits she had never thought possible, or even existed.

She wanted desperately to cry out, but had no sounds in her throat that would reach above a groan.

'Hold in there, ma'am!' shouted Jonas, by way of a forlorn encouragement. Alicia's only response was another grunt, another groan.

'Goin' into the bend now,' shouted Jonas again. 'Round that and we might just—'

It was in that moment, as Jonas bent his back to the next thrust of the paddle and Alicia responded with another gasp behind him, that the first thunder rolled across the peaks like a bad-tempered growl.

The black clouds closed to a mass, thunder rolled again, lightning cracked like the flash of naked flame and the rain cut loose in a torrential downpour.

Jonas lifted his creased, grimacing face to the skies, uncertain of whether the storm had come as a saviour or crashed across the dawn like a tormentor. Either way the faint light faded as if doused.

Now they were into a sudden gloom with the rain like a curtain of mist swirling across it.

'Hell!' cursed Jonas, finally risking a backward glance to check on the pursuing Cheyenne. They had made fast water, but were still too far short to close for the pincer attack and, like Jonas, were confronted now by the half light, the pouring rain and a flow that had turned from a gently deep surface to an angry rush.

He risked a quick glance at Alicia, catching her eye, the anguish, pain, fear. He smiled ruefully, but could summon nothing that would make any sense.

Jonas had turned back to the effort of paddling and trying to hold the canoe to a steady course against the whipping downpour, the lightning-streaked gloom, when he became conscious of the

sheer rock faces to his left easing away to a rocky
shoreline as they went into the bend.

But it was not the bend, the storm, the downpour, or even the Cheyenne that gripped his
already knotted stomach and turned his sweat
ice-cold. It was what he could see ahead through
the curtain of grey that chilled him.

At some time during the long bitter winter a
storm had uprooted a handful of old pines at the
water's edge and tossed them crashing across the
flow in a tight unyielding wall of trunks, tangled
branches and the clutter of scrub and flotsam
shifting downstream on the floods of the melting
snows.

Moving upstream against the barrier in the
hope of making it to Riverbend looked to be
impossible, thought Jonas in his first rain-washed
sight of it. Just as grim a reality was the fact that
the approaching *Ada Benson* would be unable to
pass beyond it. And if the captain happened to be
a greenhorn to the wiles of the Big Muddy. . . .

'Mr Jonas!'

'I see it, ma'am,' shouted Jonas to Alicia's groan
and without turning to her. 'I see it well enough.'

'We surely can't—'

'No, ma'am, you're probably right – we surely
can't. But we still got them Cheyenne chasin' our
butts, so we push on. And fast!' And just to
emphasise the point he plunged the paddle to the
skimming flow with an added determination.

Jonas spat and spluttered the driving rain from
his face, gritted his teeth and peered hard ahead.
There was little enough of the detail of the barrier
to see; only the tangled, jumbled mass, the clus-

ters of dripping flotsam and snow-flood debris, every yard of the barrier a lethal trap to certain drowning for whoever came to be caught in it.

But there had to be some hope, some chance, somewhere.

He risked another backward glance to track the Cheyenne. Still there, still coming on; four bucks, two to each canoe, their bodies gleaming, muscles rippling, gazes firm and fixed; their concentration unwavering. Only a matter of time now before their greater strength outran, outflanked and outreached Jonas and the woman.

Even so, the Cheyenne shared the same problem: what to do at the barrier? Or were the bucks hopeful of making their strike before reaching the obstruction?

Jonas went back to his own concentration. The bows of the canoe were beginning to scythe at the first of the rough water from the barrier, added to now by the lashing rain and whipping wind. Thunder continued to roll, lightning to strike, and the light to move through a dozen shades of threatening grey.

'Mr Jonas,' yelled Alicia above the roar, 'what are we going to do? I don't see how—'

'Bring the canoe to the left, ma'am,' returned Jonas. 'We need to be nearer the bank.'

'The Cheyenne are closing. I don't. . . I don't think I can go on much longer.'

'Nearly there,' lied Jonas, searching madly now for some break, some cover, anything, anywhere in the looming barrier. 'Hold on! One last push!'

It might have been just that, a last push into the trap, the canoe capsizing, bodies toppled to the flow either to drown or fall to the grappling hands of Eagle Neck's bucks.

But their luck held as Jonas lifted the paddle clear of the surface, called to Alicia to do likewise, and gave the canoe its free-flowing head into the barrier.

It was only ever going to be a wild gamble, tossing fate to the wind in the hope that it landed face-up. The craft rushed on, caught now in the racing momentum of the drag sucking it ever closer and deeper into the jaws of the waiting tangle of branches and growth.

'Head down, ma'am!' shouted Jonas. 'We're goin' in. Just stay tight!'

The canoe crashed into the barrier, ripping at the fallen pines, grinding against sodden bark, creaking and spitting until it seemed the very fabric of it would be peeled from the structure like the skin from a fruit.

Jonas yelled and cursed. Alicia gasped and swallowed her screams, but held on, conscious only of the canoe bumping and crashing to a splintering halt and, in the next moment, of Jonas scrambling into the web of branches, the Winchester already ranging for its target.

FIFTEEN

The rifle blazed through the grey light and pouring rain, levelling on the leading Cheyenne canoe, forcing it off course as the bucks dived into cover and slewed against the racing flow.

'Get out and up here,' yelled Jonas as he reached for Alicia and dragged her, a scrambling tangle of arms and legs, from the snagged 'flying fish'. 'Just keep yuh head down and don't move!' he ordered, pushing her into the deepest cover.

The Winchester blazed again, this time the shots aimed at the second of the chasing canoes. A buck rose, his rifle levelling on Jonas, but too late as more shots spat and sizzled through the storm, throwing the Cheyenne to the river, his body tossed away as if no more than flotsam.

His companion glared for a moment, mouthed an obscenity, swung the canoe round full circle with a single plunge of his paddle and retreated downstream.

Jonas glanced quickly at Alicia who had slid like a partly beached fish to her waist in the teeming waters, her fingers wrapped as tight as claws round a sodden branch. 'You hold in there, ma'am,' he shouted. 'Yuh hear me?'

Alicia blinked through the smearing rain and spray, swallowed, gasped, but her voice when she finally found it was drowned in another burst of rapid fire from the Winchester as Jonas brought his aim to bear on the still approaching first canoe.

The two bucks had succeeded in correcting the slew against the current and thrashing wind and watched from a distance the fate of their companions, their anger glowing in their faces as the dead body had passed on a swirl of the flow.

Now they were set for a counter attack.

Paddles flashed as one, arms worked as if joined, bodies bent, backs heaved. The canoe headed through the water like a targeted spear, gathering speed with every plunge of the paddles, its wake frothing in the momentum; in one glimpse from where Jonas waited in the web of branches no more than a smudged blur against the driving rain, in the next a shafted beam of spectral light.

'Mr Jonas. . .' spluttered Alicia, spitting rain and river water. 'Have you seen. . . ?' She coughed and gasped.

'Yes, ma'am, I've seen, and I'm still seein',' said Jonas, his gaze narrowed on the racing canoe, fingers tight on the Winchester.

'These fellas sure as hell mean business.' He wiped the back of a hand across his mouth. 'But you just do like I say and keep yuh head down. We ain't done yet, not by a long shot we ain't.' He levelled the Winchester.

Alicia gulped, blinked, shook her head and shivered against the numbing cold. She tried paddling her legs, but they seemed now to be no longer a part of her, as if her body below the waist had been swept away on the surging flow.

The Cheyenne canoe came on, the bucks still bent to the rhythmic lift and fall of the paddles, the craft carving through the flow in a direct line for the fallen pines.

How close were the bucks intent on getting, wondered Jonas, licking the rain and sweat from his lips? Hell, were they planning on ramming the barrier?

'Damnit, that's just what they're goin' to do!' he mouthed seconds later, lifting the barrel of the rifle a fraction to fire a shot above the Cheyenne's heads.

But still the canoe raced on. Jonas fired another shot. He lowered the aim, but too late for a levelled shot as the craft swished suddenly to the left, came back on course and, before Jonas knew it, had crashed into the arms of protruding branches only yards from where he crouched.

He brought the Winchester into range for a blaze of shots that would at least push the bucks back if not take out one of them, and then raged on a string of curses as the rifle jammed.

'Goddamn-sonofa-bitch!' he groaned, swishing the weapon through a full circle to place the barrel in both hands and cleave the butt through the air like an axe.

A bull-shouldered, black-eyed buck sprang from the bows, the glistening blade of a knife flashing ahead of him. Alicia screamed, her eyes bulging, the fear fixing her expression in a twisted wince.

Jonas cursed again, grunted and brought the rifle round in a clubbing, bone-cracking swing

that caught the Cheyenne clean across the fore-
arm.

The buck groaned his agony, lost his balance
and crashed through the tangle of smaller
branches to the surging flow, only for his looming
bulk to be replaced by his companion rushing at
Jonas from the right.

Alicia screamed again, the echo of it dying to a
frustrated moan as she freed one hand and
clawed uselessly at empty space.

Jonas growled as he turned and crouched
against the oncoming buck. He swung the rifle;
the snarling buck stepped nimbly aside, balancing
himself on the sodden trunk, brought his own rifle
to bear in a levelled aim from the waist, and fired.

Instinct had forced Jonas to fling himself without thinking from a direct line with the buck to
his left, slipping instantly into the scrambling
mass of branches and flotsam, through them and
down to the flow as the blaze from the rifle roared
over him.

The buck moved, conscious for a moment of
Alicia clinging to the branch, but intent only on
stepping softly, tentatively along the pine trunk in
search of Jonas, the rifle barrel probing ahead of
him like an antennae.

He had taken no more than four shuffling steps
when a hand reached from the depths like a
tentacle to lock on his ankle and snaffle him into
the flow.

The buck spat, tried to twist and kick himself free,
could do nothing against the tightening grip on

his ankle and fell, the rifle spinning from his hold as he hit first the branches and flotsam and then the river.

Jonas loosened his grip, pushed himself clear and brought both arms into thrashing action. A roll of thunder seemed to split into vivid lightning above his head; the rain crashed in torrents, pitting his skin as if doused with hot pebbles. The buck squirmed, snarled, reached with both hands for Jonas's head, his thumbs twitching and stiffening for the chance to gouge at his eyes.

'Sonofa-hell-fire-bitch!' groaned Jonas, turning like a hooked fish in one last effort to plunge a fist into the buck's face. 'Goddamnit if I ain't had just about all I can—'

And then the fist went home with the shuddering smash of rock into sodden weed.

The buck moaned, fell back, his body already disappearing below the surface. Jonas lunged after him, the flow pounding at his chest. The fist flashed again, a third time until the blood was pouring from the Cheyenne's face, his eyes glazing, limbs as limp as broken fronds.

Jonas pushed the body into the rush of the current and propelled himself to where Alicia lay slumped semi-conscious across the branches.

'Feel the same way m'self, ma'am,' he murmured, easing her from the tangle. 'Let's get yuh out of this and into somewhere—' He turned his face to the still storm-heavy sky and lashing rain. 'Yeah, well, I ain't too certain about that right now. . . .'

SIXTEEN

He carried her, slipping and sliding over the rain-washed ground, from the river to the cover of low pine branches and a narrow overhang of rock, the storm still rolling round him, the light greyer, murkier like a giant's dirty breath.

'Best we got for now, lady,' he murmured, making her as comfortable as he could, watching her face for the merest flicker of awareness. 'But we ain't got long,' he continued, talking to himself. 'I'm goin' back to get the canoe, right, then we push on? Can't waste any more time messin' with Cheyenne!'

He licked his lips and blinked rapidly to clear the rain and river water from his eyes. 'Let's hope Eagle Neck's had enough for now. Meantime. . . .'

He sighed. 'Yeah, meantime we got Birdboy and Zackman waitin' at Riverbend and, a whole sight more important, we've got them out there waitin' wide as gapin' jaws, damn it.' He gazed at the fallen pine trunks spanning the tumbling flow. 'And the *Ada Benson* headin' straight for 'em.'

His gaze narrowed for a moment. If Zackman and Birdboy were already at Riverbend, they must have passed and seen the barrier, so what had they made of it, he wondered? Would they try to remove it or use it to their advantage?

He grunted. 'Don't you go strayin' now, ma'am,' he murmured, brushing the bedraggled hair from Alicia's brow. 'Take it easy 'til I get back. Two shakes of a steer's tail.'

He slid away to the downpour and the roaring river.

Close on another full hour had passed by the time Jonas had recovered the canoe, checked thoroughly there were no tracking Cheyenne in the vicinity and made his tired, bone-weary way back to the shelter beneath the overhang.

The rain had eased, the storm rumbled away to the south, the sky broke to a fitful light and, much to his relief, Alicia regained consciousness and something of her composure when he sat himself carefully at her side and watched her struggle against the discomfort of sodden clothes.

'Would light a fire, help yuh dry out, ma'am, if I dare,' he said with a faint shrug. 'Can't take the risk,' he added bluntly. 'Can't see any of Eagle Neck's bucks, but that don't say they ain't about. And 'sides, we need to push on. Time ain't with us.'

'What about. . . .' murmured Alicia, stifling a shiver before stiffening sharply. 'What about you? The river . . . the killings . . . those Cheyenne?' She shivered again and glanced at him quickly. 'And don't tell me—'

'I ain't tellin' yuh nothin', ma'am. There ain't the time for one thing, and for another yuh saw as well as I did what happened. Fact is, we're through this far, and there's a whole lot still waitin' on us at Riverbend.'

'Do you think—?' began Alicia again.

'I aint much for thinkin' right now, ma'am. Like yourself, I'm wet, cold, a whole heap miserable and if it weren't for the thought of some warmth and a square meal aboard the *Ada Benson*, I'd be all for lightin' that fire and to hell with it!'

'It was the boat I was about to mention. How is it going to—?'

'Get through that barrier, ma'am? I wouldn't know at this moment, but I guess Zackman and Birdboy have been givin' it some careful thought. You bet they have.'

'Supposing—'

'On your feet, lady,' ordered Jonas, offering a hand as he stood up and flexed his legs against the clinging damp. 'T'ain't goin' to be no bed of roses in the canoe, but the old flyin' fish is still in one piece and mebbe we'll dry out with the effort of shiftin' her.' He glanced into the breaking sky. 'Sun'll be up soon. That'll help. Yuh ready?'

The flow upstream of the obstruction was deeper, wider and, as the storm continued to roll on and the rain to ease and finally clear on the fresher skies, a whole sight calmer to the lift and fall of paddles.

Jonas held to a steady pace, maintaining progress without taxing the already frail strength of the woman. Alicia, for her part, stayed silent, thoughtful but concentrated on the river, the passing banks – where every shadow seemed to her to shift and follow – and the passage ahead.

She was under no illusions now as to what to expect as they neared Riverbend. But she had learned, much to her own surprise, not to probe too deeply into Jonas's thinking, or to query his plan – if, she reflected on a sudden shiver, he had one.

She had dismissed the thought on another plunge of the paddle and gone back to watching the shadows.

Jonas had been watching the one skirting the narrow track to his right for the past half-hour. Fellow was persistent if not overly smart, he concluded, bringing the canoe to the mid-stream depths. One of Zackman's trailing eyes for sure.

'Company to your right, ma'am, in case yuh ain't spotted him,' he called over his shoulder. 'No danger, just trackin'. Means Birdboy knows we're on the river and where we're headin'. Mebbe even figured our thinkin'. He'll make a move for us before the *Ada Benson* hits the bend.'

'And what shall we be doin', Mr Jonas?' asked Alicia, a dark frown furrowing her brow. 'I don't see how—'

'Neither do I, ma'am. Not right now, I don't.'

Alicia was not sure whether to believe him or not.

The flow was still holding its depth a mile short of the start of the loop to the slow meander. And it was at this point that Jonas switched his concentration from the tracking shadow to the river ahead.

If the *Ada Benson* had left Fort Bragg on schedule and made steady passage downriver, she would hit the meander by mid-afternoon, proceed gently, easily, at a reduced speed, passing clear of Riverbend to pick up the pace on what her captain would assume to be a clear run to reach Cripple Creek by sundown.

She had to be stopped, Alicia Furneaux got aboard and the captain warned of the hazards ahead – and not least those lurking at Riverbend – long before a course was set for the Creek.

'We'll get to movin' a mite faster from here, ma'am,' he called on a long plunge of his paddle. 'Riverbend comin' up on your right. We'll close on the bank to the left. Some shade there and we'll be out of rifle range. Should have the *Ada Benson* in sight in under the hour. Yuh fit for it, ma'am? Feelin' better?'

'The sun's helped me dry out some,' answered Alicia. 'I'll cope. But what I still don't understand is how—'

'Chances are I don't myself, ma'am,' clipped Jonas. 'So let's save the breath for the paddlin', shall we?'

They fell to a silence broken only by the swish of paddles and drift of the flow.

They closed on what passed for the settlement of Riverbend at an even, uninterrupted pace, Jonas hugging the far bank and the scattering of shadows for as long as the depth and current would allow.

He glanced only hurriedly at what he could make out of the activity at the bend: a curl of smoke from a long-abandoned, tumbledown trapper's shack, a line of loose-hitched mounts, the blurred shape and shadow of what might have been somebody watching from a mound of rocks, but nothing of Birdboy or Zackman.

And no shots across their bows, thought Jonas, on a soft grunt.

'It seems very quiet over there, Mr Jonas,' said Alicia, her gaze tight on the settlement, her frown deepening. 'They must have seen us. They knew we were coming.'

'Oh, they've seen us sure enough, ma'am,' answered Jonas. 'They ain't no fools. And they ain't blind neither!'

'So why are they letting us pass, do you suppose?'

Jonas was silent for a moment, his concentration settled on the momentum of the paddles. 'That, ma'am,' he said at last, 'is beginnin' to bother me.'

'You say we're out of range?'

'Well out of range, but they've had more than enough time and warnin' to get men to this side. They could have sprung a trap easy enough.'

'But they haven't, so what do you deduce from that? Are we to be allowed free passage?' She plunged a determined paddle. 'You said their whole plan of taking the gold depended on holding me to ransom. Well,' she added, on a toss of her hair, 'they haven't taken me, I'm not for being bartered. They appear to be throwing their chances to the wind.'

'Would seem like it, ma'am, savin' that it ain't ever been in Zackman's nature to quit, and I wouldn't be for bankin' on Birdboy wastin' his time this far for nothin'.' He took a firmer grip on the paddle. 'Fact is, though, ma'am, the *Ada Benson* ain't goin' no place while ever that barrier's blockin' the river.'

'You mean, they could hold up the boat here until—'

'Yes, ma'am, I mean just that.'

The flow swung to the loop and meander, broadened and began to shallow at the banks.

'All the deep water's mid-stream, ma'am, and that's our course.'

A half-hour later, Riverbend was out of view and the swish and fall of paddles had been deadened on the blasts of the *Ada Benson's* warning whistle.

SEVENTEEN

'An extraordinary story, Mr – did I hear you right when you said – Jonas? Quite remarkable. It would take some believin' if I hadn't heard it from the horse's mouth, as it were, beggin' your pardon. Yessir, some believin'.'

Oliver Furneaux, owner and first president of the St Louis and Illinois State Bank, drew heavily on his cigar to release a thick cloud of smoke across the ornately and expensively furnished saloon lounge of the *Ada Benson*. He glanced quickly at his daughter seated at his side, and smiled gently.

His gaze moved on to the lavishly dressed and pomaded man with an arm across Alicia's shoulders and a look approaching disdain on his clean-shaven face. 'My partner here, Mr Harley Wensum, agrees, don't you, Harley? said Furneaux.

'Of course,' replied Wensum, almost sneering the word, his eyes on Jonas unblinking. 'You did well, Mr Jonas. We are grateful to you.'

'Say that again,' boomed Furneaux, behind another cloud of smoke which he wafted clear of

his face. 'Hadn't been for what you did out there
for my daughter, for this tub of a boat, damn it,
why I shudder to think. . . . Don't bear contemplatin'.'

Jonas wheeled his hat nervously through his
hands, settling his gaze equally self-consciously
on the woman. One hell of a transformation there,
he thought, admiring once again the dress Alicia
had changed into after bathing and resting up.
Two hours aboard the *Ada Benson* had restored
her from a sodden, bedraggled, dirt and mud-
smeared wreck to – to a St Louis banker's daughter, mused Jonas on a slow grunt and faint smile.

Alicia returned the smile and stiffened slightly
at the touch of the man at her side.

'But the fact of the matter is,' began Furneaux
again, 'we are still in somethin' of a dilemma.
Ain't that so, McBright?' He turned through the
smoke to the tall, weathered, neatly uniformed
captain of the steamer standing at the door.

'No denyin' to that, sir,' said the skipper in a
rich, throaty brogue. 'It is, as you say, a remarkable story, and I'm as grateful as any for what Mr
Jonas has done, but the truth of it is I can't stay
anchored here in the meanders for much longer.
Somehow, somebody, or something, has got to
remove that obstruction downriver. We must,
absolutely must, pass on to Cripple Creek to
refuel.'

'Meantime,' coughed Furneaux, eyeing the
glowing tip of his cigar accusingly, 'we've got a
heap of scumbags threatenin' us at Riverbend, it
seems, and a Cheyenne chief with a mean streak
who ain't goin' to settle for anythin' less, I suspect,

than blood and the prized trophy of my daughter.'

He coughed again and fastened the cigar between his fat, gold-ringed fingers. 'I'm a realist, Mr Jonas, see things black and white – shades of grey can wait – so what I want an answer to is this: how are we goin' to shift this tub from here, past Riverbend, through that barrier and on to Cripple Creek? You know the nature of our cargo, you've seen what men will do to get their hands on it – that's gold for yuh – but you seem to me to be a man of some resource. And that, right now, is exactly what I need.'

The banker fixed Jonas with a piercing gaze. 'What yuh say, Mr Jonas? Would you have a plan for gettin' out of this? Would you have any ideas? Damnit, what I'm sayin' is plain enough, ain't it? I'm askin' if you'll help us once more.' He raised a hand. 'I know, it could be said you've done enough, but I'm askin' best way I know how. Name your price.'

Furneaux drew on the cigar again and blew a perfectly formed circle of smoke to the ceiling. 'Somebody's sold me gut-achin' short over this particular venture,' he murmured darkly. 'Somebody I'll get to, don't you fret – when we've reached Cripple Creek.' He blew another smoke circle, waited until its edges were shimmering, then broke it on a sudden breath. 'How we goin' to do it, Mr Jonas? Tell me.'

Jonas steadied his hat in his hands, shifted a leg against the itch of the dry pants he had been offered on coming aboard, a shoulder on the tightness of the clean shirt, and glanced from Captain

McBright, to Oliver Furneaux, Harley Wensum, and then to Alicia, whose eyes on him were as tight as a beam.

'Only one way it can be done,' he said quietly.

'I'm listenin', Mr Jonas,' urged Furneaux. 'Speak your mind and don't give no thought to the cost.'

McBright stiffened as if about to face bad weather. Wensum's gaze on Jonas turned colder. Alicia began to frown.

'Blow it up,' said Jonas bluntly. 'Dynamite them fallen pines downriver clean out of the water, or sufficient of 'em through the deep water for safe passage for the boat. Ain't no other way.'

Furneaux turned brusquely to McBright. 'Well,' he asked, 'could it be done? Would that be enough? Are we carryin' dynamite?'

The captain steadied his broad shoulders. 'We're carryin' dynamite, and, yes, it could be done, but I'm just not certain how—'

'How many men would you need, Mr Jonas?' snapped Furneaux.

'I ain't said nothin' about doin' it,' said Jonas flatly.

'No, you ain't,' clipped the banker on a grin and a surge of smoke, 'but I got one hell of a gut feelin' you will!'

Alicia shifted her hands in her lap. Wensum's fingers flexed on her shoulder. McBright's eyes gleamed anxiously beneath the vastness of his bushy eyebrows.

Jonas waited a moment, silent, staring blankly, his thoughts spinning through a whirl of images: the early morning sight of the tracking Cheyenne on the banks of the Big Muddy, the three riders and the captured woman, Birdboy, the shack, the dash for the river, the bodies, smell of blood, dead bodies, lingering cordite, the pounding storm and the struggle with Eagle Neck's bucks, Alicia Furneaux clinging desperately to the debris of fallen pines and flotsam. . . .

'I go alone,' said Jonas, his stare flaring to a steel-bright gaze.

'Alone?' murmured the captain.

'You heard the man,' said Furneaux, coughing on a surge of cigar smoke.

'But I've got men aboard, good, solid men, trustworthy,' began McBright again. 'I'd rate any one of them.' He slapped his lips. 'This ain't a job for one man.'

Harley Wensum slid his arm from Alicia's shoulders and crossed to the saloon's drinks cabinet where he poured himself a large whiskey.

'Mr Jonas appears to me to be a man who knows his own mind,' he said, turning from the cabinet, glass in hand, a wry grin breaking his clean lips. 'If he says he goes alone, then I am sure he means just that, although I for one would be fascinated to hear just how he plans to do it.'

He sipped carefully on the drink and raised his eyebrows on his gaze into Jonas's eyes.

McBright sighed to hide a grunt of annoyance. Furneaux wafted at smoke and glared at the tip of the cigar. Alicia's fingers twisted anxiously in her lap; her eyes narrowed, the frown deepened.

'No master plannin',' said Jonas lightly, wheeling his hat again. 'I've got the canoe; I sneak out of here at dusk, head downriver, reach the barrier, set the dynamite and blow it. Captain McBright could have the boat underway come first light.'

'As simple as that?' mocked Wensum.

'You wanna make it complicated?' frowned Jonas.

'I was wondering, just as a matter of interest, you understand,' shrugged Wensum sarcastically, 'how you might cope alone, for example, with any of Eagle Neck's marauding bucks, or, how you would handle the men awaiting us at Riverbend?' He sipped at the drink again. 'Although I'm sure you've considered these possibilities.'

'Eagle Neck's bucks won't move at night,' said Jonas. 'As for Birdboy and Zackman, well, I guess I'll just have to steer well clear of Riverbend, won't I?'

'Sounds fine to me,' blustered Furneaux. 'What yuh say, McBright, you go along with Mr Jonas's reckonin'?'

'There is very little choice,' said the captain.

'Then we're agreed,' beamed Furneaux. 'Your way, Mr Jonas. You got it. You'll do it?'

Apple pie, clean sheets, a decent bed, thought Jonas, smiling softly to himself. 'Why not?' he murmured. 'I ain't got no other place to be.'

EIGHTEEN

The flow lapped gently at the canoe's bows; the light lay dappled across the dark surface of the water; two eyes watched with all the alertness and intensity of a muskrat. The only sounds from the night-shrouded pine forest were of four-legged hunters in search of their prey – and the scurrying prey in their bid for survival.

Jonas waited, his breathing easy, gaze tight, uncertain now of whether he was the hunter or the hunted.

He held the craft steady at the bankside, one hand gripping the anchorage of a fallen pine branch, the other still firm on the paddle. He figured his luck was holding. He was alone.

He dared to blink and relaxed. He was doing well enough, he reckoned. Passage from the *Ada Benson* had been fast and silent through the depths of the night.

'You'll find enough draught for one man and a light canoe to starboard,' McBright had murmured as Jonas had taken his place in the craft. 'Stay close to the shoreline. Maximum shadow. Dynamite's been stowed forward. Keep it dry whatever you do. Pick you up downriver soon after sun-up – God willing. Good luck. Oh, and thanks.'

The captain's smile had been wide, warm and confident, but it had taken some summoning, Jonas had thought.

His last view of the *Ada Benson* as he had slipped away into the darkness had been of McBright, a cigar-puffing Furneaux and the preening Harley Wensum watching from the deck-rails amidships.

Not until the last glimmer of the steamboat's lights had he caught a glimpse of Alicia standing apart from the others in the pale yellow glow of the saloon's trimmed lamps. She had raised a hand nervously as if to wave, lowered it equally nervously to finger her neck, tossed her hair across her shoulders and disappeared into the saloon.

He could only wonder what he might have seen in her eyes.

Jonas steadied the canoe again, murmuring softly under his breath, cleared his mind of images and concentrated on his immediate surroundings.

He had left the *Ada Benson* far behind and drawn level on the opposite bank to the shack at Riverbend where Zackman, Birdboy and their guns were holed up. The flow was flat but still full after the surge of mountain waters brought down on the storm, and doubtless adding to the clutter of the flotsam at the barrier. He would need to approach with care, he decided, especially with the added hazard of darkness.

But not before he had established as best he

could from here just what was happening at the Riverbend shack.

He pushed clear of his anchorage and paddled softly out to the faster flow, hugging the deepest darkness against the passage of a restless moon, edging as close as he dared to the rocky shoreline of Riverbend.

The shack lay in darkness without so much as the glimmer of a glow at the window; no sounds either of hitched mounts; no guards posted; no dozing look-outs scanning the river. All quiet. Nothing.

So were Zackman and Birdboy lying low, staying silent, waiting on first light to make their move, waiting perhaps for the captain of the *Ada Benson* to make his move?

Or had they, wondered Jonas on a deeper grunt to himself, moved upriver to keep a close eye on the steamboat through the night; to be there almost at her side, when the *Ada Benson*'s boilers came to life again and she pounded downriver intent on ramming the barrier?

Or were they already at the barrier?

Jonas slowed the craft and turned her slowly, carefully back to the shadow-filled opposite bank. He would keep moving now, slowly, silently, maintaining a steady pace, hugging the darkness, staying on the blank side of the moon, slipping through its light like a stray shadow.

He would be there in an hour.

The flow quickened out of the long drift of the loop and began to swirl in the drag of the barrier. Jonas eased the canoe back on a full plunge of the paddle that slewed him sharply left, then right on a swish of the way as the bows cut at the flow, and came head-on again. He licked at a sudden beading of cold sweat and tightened his grip.

The barrier loomed like a sliver of stranded black cloud, the branches from the main trunks twisting into the light as if from a shredded web, the flotsam clinging and dripping in globules of dark.

Jonas swallowed, steadied the canoe again and brought it gently into the growth at the bank some yards short of the bulk. He secured the craft, unloaded the dynamite, checked that he had fastened his hunting knife in his belt, and crouched low, waiting, watching.

He listened to the drift of the flow, its tumble and gurgle through the gaps in the barrier, the startled clatter of a disturbed roosting bird, the echoing call of a distant animal.

Otherwise, just another long night on the Big Muddy.

He shivered a touch as he slid to the flow and, keeping the dynamite well clear of the water, made his slow way to the central point of the barrier. He would plan the main explosion in the thickest area, two others to left and right, with any luck clearing a passage for the *Ada Benson* at the river's deepest sprawl.

He reached the central point and worked quickly, silently, his concentration fixed, his touch assured in the fluttering light. Given an uninterrupted hour, he reckoned he could be all through before—

It was then that something, from somewhere, smashed across his shoulders like a slab of rock.

*

Jonas groaned, lost his grip and floundered from the barrier to disappear below the surface for vital, splashing seconds as he fought against the numbing pain and ice-cold depths.

He came splutteringly back to the moonlight, spewing river water, his head reeling, but his eyes already tight on the looming bulk and leering grin of the man straddling the barrier above him.

'Caught up with yuh at last, eh, mister?' sneered the man, spitting across the flow. 'Birdboy figured I would if I waited around long enough.' His fingers closed on the length of broken branch at his side. 'You want another taste of this, or are yuh for comin' quiet? Suit yourself. I ain't in no hurry – but you've sure as hell been wastin' your time here, fella!'

Jonas shook his head, blinked, trod water to stay afloat and upright. He glared at the man through the moonlit gloom. 'Where's that sono-fabitch Birdboy, right now?' he croaked.

'Well, now,' grinned the man, 'wouldn't you just like to know that? Why, I figure we could spend the whole of this night discussin' the matter and yuh still wouldn't be any—'

Jonas had given the man the space to talk, watched his grip on the branch relax again, his fixed stare begin to weaken, his straddled body ease, before his right hand sprang from below the surface gripping the knife he had pulled from his belt and slashed into the sidekick's leg.

There was an agonizing scream, a groaned, gurgled string of curses, a spurt of blood, and then the man had lost his hold and balance and crashed to the flow.

Jonas plunged the knife again as the man flayed his arms wildly, this time raising more blood from a slash across the sidekick's shoulder.

The man rolled, crazed now with pain and anger. 'Damn yuh eyes!' he cursed, flinging himself at Jonas like some flow-tossed log. 'Damned if I don't kill yuh outright – and right now!'

In spite of his wounds, the seeping blood, the drag of the current, the cold and snagging traps of the barrier, the man lunged again, both hands springing open like claws ready to fasten on whatever they reached.

Jonas took a deep breath and plunged below the surface, slipping the knife from his grip, but grabbing the man's left leg and yanking it violently, then locking his fingers on it until it seemed drained of life.

Jonas sprang back to the surface, his hands locking on the weakened man's throat. 'I asked you where Birdboy is now,' he spluttered, 'and I don't recall gettin' an answer. So where is the sonofabitch?'

The man flayed, groaned, spat, blood swimming round him like scarlet light.

Jonas tightened his grip. 'Where is he?'

The man opened his mouth on what might have been a curse telling Jonas to go to hell, but thought better of it as a boot smashed agonizingly into his wounded leg.

'He's on the *Ada Benson*, damn yuh,' he groaned, under the throttling pressure of Jonas's grip. 'Him and Zackman. They all are.'

The cold cling of the river seemed to eat into Jonas at that moment. 'What yuh mean, on the *Ada Benson*? How come?'

'We guessed yuh hadn't figured that,' scoffed the man on a dribble of blood from the corner of his mouth. 'Hadn't reckoned on it, had yuh? The woman's fiancé, Wensum, he's back of this whole thing. It's his set-up.'

The man summoned every last ounce of his failing strength to thrash a fist into the side of Jonas's head. Jonas winced and lashed out, his own fist smashing full into the man's face as a sudden surge of the flow dragged him out of sight and into the depths of the darkness.

Jonas shuddered and struck out for the safety of the bank, too stunned, sodden and exhausted to think straight, his only concern to reach dry land.

NINETEEN

He blew the barrier at dawn.

The final decision, in the light of what he had learned, had not been taken easily. The physical task of going back to the icy flow in the darkness to set the dynamite had been just as difficult, but the odds against Alicia, her father, Captain McBright and the crew of the *Ada Benson* staying alive if they were to remain stranded in the meanders far outweighed any personal concerns.

'And 'sides,' he had murmured to himself with a shudder on the chill of the night through sodden clothes, 'I got some scores to settle. . . .'

Birdboy and Zackman had come quickly to mind, but what of Harley Wensum, he wondered, who was going to settle the score with him: Alicia Furneaux, the woman he was supposed to be marrying; her father, the president of the bank in which Wensum had become a partner; Captain McBright, whose steamboat he had seized? And how many others lurking in his past life?

And what would happen to the gold?

If the *Ada Benson* stayed anchored in the meanders, it would take days and many hands to unload the cargo to the difficult shoreline and then transport it overland to wherever Wensum intended it to come to rest. There were too many risks involved in such a plan.

No, Jonas had decided, Wensum would want to move the gold to where he had originally planned for the heist to take place, with Alicia Furneaux as the ransom: at Cripple Creek.

So, he had resolved, he would clear the way, dynamite the barrier as intended, open a passage for Captain McBright to bring the steamboat safely through and set fair and uninterrupted for Cripple Creek.

What might await Wensum and his men there, of course, was something nobody could predict.

The barrier had blown in a flying mass of timber, debris and flotsam high into an already early sun-streaked sky, raining across the light like the flight of a million varieties of scattering birds, butterflies and moths. The explosion would have been heard for miles, thought Jonas on a satisfied smile, as he waited for the first rush and gush of water to settle through the newly cleared flow-path.

More than wide enough for the passage of the *Ada Benson*, he reckoned, with most of the loose flotsam and debris cleared by the time the boat reached this section.

He had waited another half-hour before settling himself to the canoe again and paddling softly, silently away, downriver in the direction of Cripple Creek. The morning was already turning warm on the rising sun; the shadows were long and deep, the silence almost unbroken, and the Big Muddy at peace with itself.

A perfect time of day and setting to begin plotting retribution, Jonas had thought.

'I will say this once and once only, Harley Wensum,' growled Oliver Furneaux across the smoke and liquor-hazed saloon of the *Ada Benson*, 'you will be brought to book for this and, if I have my way, surely hang – long and high, damn you!'

The bank president squirmed against the ropes binding him to the chair facing the two men watching him. 'And another thing,' he went on, eyes bulging, nostrils flaring, 'if you're reckonin' for one minute that you're going to get away with this—'

'I think you've had more than your say for now,' said Wensum, with a mean sidelong glance as he crossed to the saloon window and stared into the slowly lifting dawn.

'Leave it, Pa,' urged Alicia from the chair at his side. She winced at the burn of the rope at her wrists and tossed her hair dramatically.

'Thank you, my dear,' grinned Wensum, without turning. 'I see you are beginning to register some sense after your wild escapade. And very welcome it is too.'

'Don't fool yourself, Harley,' snapped Alicia. 'When this is over—'

'Which it will be very soon, my dear, and when it is, you will have a simple enough choice.'

'You lay a finger on my daughter. . .' blustered Furneaux.

Wensum turned slowly, the grin on his face fading to the grey line of his mouth. 'Your daughter, Oliver, will do precisely as I say, when I say, or suffer the consequences. As you will yourself when I give the orders. You are not in a bargaining position, either of you. Best that you come to terms with the reality of your situation, and do so right now.'

'You want I should quieten one of these whelps?' drawled Zackman, rolling a wad of chewing tobacco round his mouth. 'But not the woman, eh? Don't want her spoiled yet.'

Alicia stiffened and tossed her hair again.

Furneaux swallowed, almost choked but managed, 'I'll see the pair of you in Hell. . .' before he finally did choke and splutter into silence.

'You'll do nothing, Mr Zackman,' ordered Wensum, gripping the lapels of his brocaded frock coat. 'You'd best look to Birdboy out there on the bridge with Captain McBright, make sure this boat negotiates the barrier Mr Jonas has so kindly cleared for us and steams at full speed for the Creek. I want to be there before nightfall.'

'Real decent of that Jonas fella blowin' the barrier like that,' grinned Zackman. 'Hell, if he ain't bettin' on a hiding' to nothin'—'

'Just do as I say!' glared Wensum. 'Leave these people to me.'

Zackman shrugged, rolled the wad of tobacco on a sucking of saliva, and left the saloon.

'You're mad,' groaned Oliver Furneaux. 'Stark-raving, hound-dog mad. Why in the name of tarnation—'

'Don't even begin to ask,' sneered Wensum, stepping closer as his hands fell from his lapels. 'You with your God-almighty fine bank, your wealth, your status, strutting like some damned peacock through St Louis, fixing for me to marry your lily-livered, smart-butt daughter and making me a so-called partner just to get your own way with things same as you always have.' He spat defiantly across the saloon floor. 'And me there working all the goddamn hours you dictated – well, forget it, Oliver-sonofabitch-Furneaux, I'm making my own life from here on in, and with your money!'

The sweat dripped like melting ice as he bent lower to stare directly into the banker's eyes. 'Every last grain of the gold dust aboard this belching tub is mine. And if you so much as murmur a breath of dissent or lift a finger against me, she, your beloved Alicia, gets handed out to Birdboy and his men.' He stepped back. 'Do I make myself one-hundred-and-one-per cent crystal clear, Mr President?'

Alicia's eyes had closed on the chill that was icing her spine. Oliver Furneaux could only swallow as if digesting something vile. The *Ada Benson's* whistle shrilled loud and clear across the morning and the Big Muddy parted to her thrusting bows.

'We are making good progress, don't you think?' grinned Harley Wensum.

It was deep into the afternoon of that same day, still cloudless, sunlit and for the most part silent, when Jonas paddled the canoe into a pine-shadowed inlet some miles short of Cripple Creek.

He was tired, his arms and shoulders almost groaning under the effort of steering and paddling the canoe without stopping since leaving the debris of the barrier. But it had been vital to keep going, he had decided.

Assuming the *Ada Benson* to have been under the control of Wensum, Zackman and Birdboy since sometime during the previous night, and that McBright had been ordered to get underway within minutes of hearing the shuddering explosion, it would surely be Wensum's plan to maintain maximum knots in his hurry to reach Cripple Creek and trigger whatever arrangements he had in position there for unloading the gold dust to its onward journey.

Keeping clear water ahead of the pounding steamboat had near-exhausted Jonas's already weary body. Even so, he had made it to the inlet with the *Ada Benson* still not in sight and only the echoing call and blast of her ringing in his ears.

He jumped to the bank, dragging the canoe into the shadowed brush, collected the restored Winchester and spare ammunition he had carried from the boat, and scurried quickly to the edge of the narrow track that twisted away towards Cripple Creek.

He reckoned another hour at least of steady progress on foot before he reached town, and only then if he managed to stay clear of any of Eagle Neck's marauding bucks. It would be dusk by the time he came to the main street leading to the deep-water dock. It was here that the *Ada Benson* would berth.

Would Wensum unload the gold through the night? Who would he be unloading it to? Where would it be heading, by what means: wagons with outriders, or in the saddle-bags of trusted side-kicks? How many town men did Wensum have in his pay? Was Sheriff Calpott among them? And what would be the fate of Alicia Furneaux, her father, and Captain McBright? Did he need to ask?

He was ahead of the steamboat's echoing whistle by barely a handful of miles as he took to the track.

Jonas slid through the shadows like a dark cat. He passed from the depths of a deserted alley to the shadowed doorway of a closed store in one moment, to the jumbled maze of crates, barrels, boxes, stacked sacks of wheat and maize cluttering the dimly lit dockside in the next. And he went without a sound.

The town had been relatively quiet on his arrival from the pine-wood track, the hum of expectancy and anticipation surrounding the approach of the *Ada Benson* being confined to the bustling saloon and the few groups of men waiting on the dock in the hope of casual work. There had been no sign, save for the glow of a lantern in the window of his office, of Sheriff Calpott or his deputies; only a handful of lounging bystanders, a trio of bar girls taking the fresher air, a night drunk already sleeping it off, a clutch of hitched mounts, a baleful dog. The only sounds had come from the tinkling piano in the bar, the buzz of voices, a woman's drunken giggles.

Full night would be settled deep by the time the *Ada Benson* was finally docked, Jonas had decided, crouching low in the shadows among the bulks of the wooden warehouses fronting the river.

He would wait and watch and stay silent – just like a cat.

TWENTY

Bells clanged, footfalls thudded, orders were shouted, voices called across the fading light; the thud and pound of the *Ada Benson's* engines began to ease, the great paddle-wheels to swish to a halt. The Big Muddy churned and the dock-side at Cripple Creek came to bustling life amid a sudden glow of newly primed and lit lanterns.

Harley Wensum watched the activity from the saloon window, a smug, satisfied smile creasing his clean-shaven face, his fingers twitching anxiously over the soft lapels of his coat and frills of his fancy shirt.

'Well, now,' he said, turning to Oliver Furneaux and Alicia still roped to their chairs, 'that all seems most satisfactory. And all right on time,' he added, consulting his silver timepiece. 'We could not have asked for more, could we?'

The bank president scowled, Alicia stiffened, her eyes round and bright and defiant.

'I could hardly expect you to agree, could I? Of course not.' The saloon door opened on Birdboy and one of his sidekicks. 'Well?' snapped Wensum irritably.

'McBright's dockin' now,' leered Birdboy. 'So

what yuh want next?' His gaze strayed over Alicia. 'I could take the woman. Get her off your hands,' he grinned.

'Don't be such a fool,' glared Wensum. 'Miss Furneaux is our most valuable asset. Tell Zackman to secure Captain McBright below decks, somewhere tight, and the same goes for those of the crew who aren't with us.' He twitched his fingers over the shirt. 'Sheriff Calpott will be coming aboard as soon as we're tied up. Send him to me the minute he arrives.'

'What about the gold?' said Birdboy, slinging his weight to one hip.

'Patience, my friend, patience,' soothed Wensum. 'That will come later.' His expression darkened. 'Any sign of that Jonas fellow?'

'He won't show again, don't you fret,' said Birdboy with an arrogant swagger.

'But there's been nothing from the man you left at the barrier. What happened to him?'

Birdboy shrugged. 'Who's to say? Fellas like him come and go on the wind. Barrier got blown, so who's worryin'?'

'The question to be asked, my dear fellow, is, *who* blew the barrier and where is he now?' Wensum consulted his timepiece again. 'Enough,' he announced. 'Get back to Zackman and secure McBright.'

Birdboy shrugged and closed the door.

'A problem?' said Alicia, when the saloon was quiet again.

'Problem?' frowned Wensum. 'We do not have problems.'

'Jonas might be a problem if he's still out there.'

Alicia's grin was mockingly cynical. '*Especially* if he's out there.'

'That's a bone-crackin' fact!' growled Furneaux.

Wensum was silent for a long moment, his expression shifting like changing light through his thoughts. 'I think not,' he grinned at last. 'But should such an unlikely possibility become a reality, then you, my dear Alicia, will have yet another role to play when I trade your life against his. I wonder what your precious Mr Jonas would decide then?' The grin broadened. 'Think about it.'

'I don't think there's much doubt about it, my dear,' said Oliver Furneaux, squirming against the rope binding him to the chair, his glance at his daughter brief and watery. 'He's goin' to kill us. He doesn't have any choice, not now. It's too late.'

The banker swallowed, sweated, winced at the burn of the rope and let his gaze move slowly, carefully round the now deserted saloon. 'I don't suppose there's a hope in hell of gettin' out of this, is there?'

Alicia smiled weakly as she flexed her fingers against the binding at her wrist. 'None I can think to, Pa,' she murmured. 'And even if we did, I don't think we'd get a step beyond that door, would we? There's one of Harley's men standing the other side of it.'

Furneaux grunted and winced again before he sighed and relaxed as far as the rope would permit. 'Who'd have thought it? Who'd have even reckoned it in their wildest dreams: Harley Wensum double-dealin' me all down the line, and me – *me* of all people – fallin' for it, every damned slice and crumb of it? Why, if I had my way. . . .' He coughed and blinked on the oozing sweat. 'And you too, my dear,' he went on quietly, 'taken in like the rest of us. Just fooled and then made to look foolish. It don't bear figurin' to, and that's the brute fact.'

He fumed a moment. 'But I'm proud of you, Alicia, and that's another fact. What you've done, tried to do along with that fella, Jonas, the spirit you've shown, the courage . . . riskin' your life out there. If that ain't somethin' to be proud of, eh? Ain't it just! I tell yuh straight up, my dear, if we get out of this in one piece. . . . Sure, that's the nub of it, *if* we get out. . . .'

There was a sudden movement, a scuffle, a stifled groan behind the closed door.

'What was that?' murmured Alicia, staring at the door. 'Did you hear it?'

'Sure, I did. Sounded to me—'

'Listen,' urged Alicia, concentrating her gaze.

Dockside voices, crunch of wagon wheels, creak and spin of a winch, but only silence behind the door. Alicia's eyes narrowed as she peered intently across the shadowy room. Had that been the sound of a soft step, she wondered? Was the door handle turning?

She swallowed, blinked, was conscious of a trickle of cold sweat down her neck.

Furneaux grunted quietly.

The sound of another step. The handle continued to turn.

And then the door was open and a body slipped through the narrow space.

*

'Mr Jonas!' hissed Alicia, her eyes wide and round.

'I'll be damned!' groaned Furneaux. 'How'd yuh manage—?'

'No time for explanations,' said Jonas, already clearing the blade of a knife from his belt. 'We move, and fast.' He cut the ropes binding Alicia's wrists, then turned to her father. 'We've got only minutes before somebody gets to checkin' on the sidekick I put to sleep out there.'

'How did you get on board?' hissed Alicia again.

'Followed the crowd, ma'am. Any amount of fellas bein' drafted aboard since McBright docked. I joined the line and kept my head down. Lucky it was dark.'

'But how the hell we goin' to get off?' murmured Furneaux squirming out of the cut ropes. 'That ain't goin' to be easy. And, damn it, Mr Jonas, you ain't even carryin' a gun.'

'Got a Winchester stashed on the dock,' said Jonas, replacing the knife. 'Couldn't come aboard with it – might have looked suspicious. The blade here is all I've got. It'll have to do.'

'What about McBright?'

'Can't get to him. Bein' held below decks. Too well guarded. 'Sides he'd never leave the *Ada Benson*, would he?' Jonas crossed back to the door. 'You follow me, right? And no sounds. Not a word. Let's go.'

Alicia checked herself against a sudden shiver. She seemed somehow to have been here before.

They were out of the saloon and into the fresher air of the night within seconds, Jonas leading them stealthily through the shadows towards the stern of the boat.

The main deck and the bows were already bustling with bodies; crewmen, Zackman and Birdboy's sidekicks, an odd assortment of the Cripple Creek roosters who made their scant livings from fuelling, loading and unloading the steamboats, Sheriff Calpott and a handful of his deputies, some lounging bar girls on the prowl for custom and, not least on this particular night, Harley Wensum at the centre of activities, his arms like windmills as he directed operations.

Jonas indicated with his right arm for them to pause a moment before scurrying on through whatever he could find of near total darkness, through a maze of ropes, a scattering of crates and barrels to the stern.

'Just what exactly do you have in mind, Mr Jonas?' hissed Furneaux from behind his daughter.

'Gettin' yourself and Miss Alicia off this boat fast as I can,' returned Jonas, his gaze piercing the darkness. 'Only minutes now before Wensum discovers you're on the loose – and then it'll be all hell from here on. He gets his hands on either one of you again, and that's it. He won't hesitate a second time about killin' you.'

'I'm not one bit concerned about the gold,' hissed Furneaux. 'Wensum and his scum can have it.'

'No, Mr Furneaux, that's just what they ain't goin' to have,' grunted Jonas. 'Not while I'm still breathin', anyhow. Come too far for that; too many died. That gold is stayin' right where it is 'til it reaches St Louis. Anythin' else ain't legal.'

Alicia smiled softly to herself for a moment, then stiffened and tapped Jonas's shoulder lightly. 'Up ahead, Mr Jonas. Somebody there at the rail. Probably a guard.'

'You got it, ma'am. Very definitely a guard. Gotta take care of him, and fast.'

'Shall I do my lure act again?' said Alicia, patting her hair into her neck.

'No, ma'am, I don't think—'

'Oh, don't be silly. How else are you going to get within striking distance of him? He's not there to make polite conversation, you know! Leave it to me, but be ready.' She slid to the night from Jonas's side.

'What in the name of tarnation is she doin'?' mouthed Furneaux on another hiss. 'She crazy or somethin'?'

'No, Mr Furneaux, that she surely ain't. You watch.'

Jonas slipped the knife from his belt and waited like a tiger tensed for its prey.

Alicia moved seductively from the shadows to a patch of light close to the rail, tossed her hair and smiled at the startled guard.

'Evening,' she murmured softly. 'Thought I'd take some air. Warm, isn't it?'

The man swallowed, ran a hand instinctively to the butt of his Colt and stared round-eyed and uncertain of what to do.

'I don't reckon,' he began. 'I mean, I ain't been told nothin' about—'

'Oh, come now,' pouted Alicia, 'you wouldn't deny a lady a breath of air, would you?' She raised her eyebrows provocatively. 'What's your price? Every man has a price.'

She raised a hand and crooked her index finger in a beckoning gesture, her smile growing warmer as the man's hand lifted from the Colt and he moved slowly towards her.

He would not have seen the shadow at his side begin to move, or had the concentration to notice how a part of it broke away as if sliced through; nor would he have been aware of the soft step, the raised arm, the flashing glint of a blade. He would have felt the plunge of the knife, heard his attacker's stifled groan of effort, but then the night would have emptied to an endless, unlit darkness.

'Well, I'll be darned, damned if I won't,' murmured Oliver Furneaux through a lathering of sweat.

Alicia stepped back as the man's body thudded to her feet and was conscious on a shiver of Jonas recovering himself from the lunge, of her father's gleaming face in the shadows, of another movement closing in a rush to her right.

She swung towards the approach of a second sidekick as Jonas steadied himself on the deck-rail, her arm swinging under the momentum of sheer survival, her clenched fist smashing viciously into the fellow's face, throwing him back. Jonas sprang like a hungry tiger, the knife-blade slashing at the man's neck. There was a single grunt, a single groan, then neither sound nor movement from the two dead bodies, sprawled in the pools of their blood.

'Snake's alive!' hissed Furneaux.

'Thanks, ma'am,' murmured Jonas, collecting a Colt and spare ammunition from one of the guards. 'Quick thinkin' there. Let's move on, fast as we can.' He guestured for Furneaux to join them as they headed deeper into the stern, the first shouts of discovery at their escape ringing in their ears.

TWENTY-ONE

'Of all the stupid, louse-ridden incompetents it has been my misfortune to have to look in the face. . . .' Harley Wensum crashed his footfalls across the saloon floor as if intent on smashing through to the lower decks, turned at the window overlooking the bows and glared at the assembled group of men. 'You realize, of course, what you've done, what *we*, all of us, have lost? We've thrown away our only bargaining piece, the woman. That's what you've done, gentlemen, thrown it away. And with it very probably the gold.'

'The gold's still here, damn it,' sneered Birdboy, lounging on one hip. 'Right under our feet.'

'Sure it is,' grinned Zackman. 'We ain't lost the gold, not no how we ain't. All we gotta do—'

'I don't need you to tell me what to do, Mr Zackman,' snapped Wensum. 'I know perfectly well what to do: we have to continue to ship this gold downriver to Marshall's Quay where we unload to wagons for the trail south and our disappearance into nowhere for a while. And in order to do that we need safe, uninterrupted passage for as long as we so choose – guaranteed for us while ever we held Alicia Furneaux. Nobody would dare to make a move that might prejudice her life.' He glared fiercely. 'You have just allowed that guarantee to slip through our fingers.'

'Now hold on there,' protested Sheriff Calpott, thrusting his thumbs into the broad belt at his considerable waist. 'I got somethin' to say on this. First, the woman, her pa and that two-bit fella they call Jonas – they won't have left Cripple Creek. And they won't neither, not tonight, not in the dark and not, as I happen to know is the case, while Eagle Neck and his bucks are all whooped up for a killin'. They'll be holed-up somewheres in town 'til at least first light.'

Calpott rolled a wad of tobacco round his mouth. 'That bein' the case,' he continued with a swelling note of authority, 'I figure we can find 'em and have the woman safe aboard this tub again in just a few hours, three at most, well before dawn. All we need is a properly organized search of the town and we'll have them slick-horners out of the woodwork easy as pickin' lice.'

He sucked noisily on the tobacco and gazed at the faces watching him.

'Well said, Sheriff,' smiled Wensum. 'You're a man after my own heart. You think things through, work it out, come to a plan of action. And that's what I like to hear. You won't go unrewarded for your efforts.' His smile faded as he glared at the others. 'Well, what are you waiting for? Get to it. Find that woman, damn you!'

Oliver Furneaux brushed a cobweb from the top of his head, winced apologetically at the creak of the stair as he followed behind Jonas and Alicia to the top floor of the dark, deserted warehouse, and blinked at the soft spread of moonlight through a dusty window.

'Own half-a-dozen places like this back in St Louis,' he wheezed in a hushed murmur. 'Never figured for havin' to hide in one.' He creaked through another step on the steep wooden stair. 'Lucky you found it, Mr Jonas, though I don't reckon it'll be long before the scumbags out there get to rummagin' for us. Seem to be makin' enough noise. Must have discovered the bodies.'

'Seems so,' grunted Jonas. 'We'll take our chances. Can't do much other.' He reached the top of the stairs, extended a hand to assist Alicia and her father, slid away to a corner of the storeroom, collected the Winchester, and then crossed to the window overlooking the quayside. He grunted again and peered closer. 'They know we're loose. Sheriff's directin' operations.'

Alicia came to his side. 'If we can hold out here 'til first light, we could maybe slip clear of the town, head back to the hills, perhaps get a message through to the marshal at Fort Bragg, or warn St Louis what's happened.' She tossed her hair angrily. 'Harley won't leave the gold, but if he tries moving out on the *Ada Benson*—'

'It's still you he needs, ma'am,' said Jonas, continuing to watch the quay. 'You're his only guarantee to shippin' out free as a bird to wherever he's got planned.'

'Country ain't big enough to hide him,' fumed Furneaux. 'Law will hunt him down sooner or later.'

'Maybe,' murmured Jonas, 'but not before him

and his rats have squandered best part of that hard-earned miners' gold, which a whole heap of folk are countin' on for their futures.'

He turned from the window and handed the Winchester to Alicia. 'Don't tell me yuh ain't got a notion how to use this, ma'am, 'cus I ain't goin' to believe yuh. You know what to do.'

'You leavin'?' frowned Furneaux.

'We just wait here, them scum'll get to us eventually, so I figure I'll take the fight to them.' Jonas spun the guard's Colt through his nimble fingers and checked out the chamber. 'Might be able to divert them from this place for long enough. You'll be safe for now, anyhow, but if needs be. . . . Well, you got the rifle. Deadly over a wide range.'

'But how—?' began Alicia, tensing.

'Like I've had good cause to say on a number of occasions these past days, ma'am, I ain't got so much as the spit of an idea, but sittin' here ain't goin' to make it one bit clearer or any easier. Best just do it.'

Alicia simply stared at him and said nothing.

Her father blinked and listened to the shouts from the quayside. Wolves howling to the hunt, he thought, coldly.

Jonas left the warehouse by the small door at the rear and slid away to the deepest shadows fronting the main street and the bustling quay. He crouched low, watched and listened to the babble of voices around him.

'You fellas there,' shouted Sheriff Calpott, waving his arms, 'get among them crates on the quayside. Examine every last one of 'em, and I mean real thorough.' He swung round. 'You – get to the livery and don't leave it. Nobody takes a horse. And you – get yourself a Winchester and position yourself top of the street. Shoot anybody tryin' to leave town. Anybody arrivin' come to that.'

Zackman sauntered to the sheriff's side. 'Me, I'll be at the saloon back there,' he drawled.

'Suit yourself,' snapped Calpott. 'Sooner we get that woman under lock and key the better for all of us.'

'Yeah, yeah, I hear yuh,' sighed Zackman, sauntering on. 'Gettin' to hear a whole lot of yuh lately.' He passed to the shadowed boardwalk.

'As for the rest of you sonsofbitches. . . .' The sheriff's shouted orders continued to fill the night as Jonas closed his ears to them and followed in the steps of the still sauntering Zackman.

He held his pace until the man had passed a narrow alley and paused on the steps back to the boardwalk to light a cigar. Jonas slipped silently into the alley, hugging the tightest of the shadows, watching the curl of smoke from the cigar. Then called the man's name in an urgent, hissing voice.

'Zackman – get yourself here.'

The gunslinger frowned behind a drift of smoke, took a step back and stared into the alley, his eyes narrowing on the seemingly empty darkness.

'Here,' hissed Jonas again.

'Who the hell are yuh?' croaked Zackman.

'Somebody you've been wantin' to see.'

The gunslinger hesitated a moment, the cigar

glowing evenly between his fingers.

'We ain't got all night.' Jonas added, a sharper edge of urgency to his voice. 'Not if you want to get to that Furneaux woman.'

Zackman edged closer into the alley, heeling the cigar as he went. 'Just who in tarnation—?'

The gleaming knife-blade slashed across the darkness like shafted light, burying itself deep into Zackman's chest. There was a grunt, a groan, a brief strengthening of the man's limbs, and then a slackening, a looseness until he crumpled at Jonas's feet and lay still.

Jonas glanced round him, watching the darkness for any movement, waiting to see if the brief scuffle had aroused attention. He dragged the body hurriedly into the depths of the alley, wiped the blade clean and slid quietly back to the shadows of the main street.

Calpott was still shouting his orders, directing men, moving from the street to the quay at an ever confusing pace as he sought to 'turn the town inside out' in the search for Alicia.

'There's gold for the first to spot her,' he bawled across the night. 'Get to it, damn yuh!'

Jonas scanned the street from the darkness. Where, he wondered, had Birdboy headed? He would not be taking his orders from Calpott, or from Wensum except when forced; he had not been with Zackman, so was he still aboard the *Ada Benson*, searching the quayside, or somewhere here on the main street?

Birdboy was no fool when it came to hiding. He would have figured instinctively that there was nowhere in town remote enough, dark enough, for

Alicia to hide for more than an hour before one of Calpott's men stumbled across her.

Jonas let his gaze wander on to the jumble of the quay and the dark mass of the warehouse where he had left Furneaux and Alicia. Would it have been to the warehouses along the quay that Birdboy's keen, scheming gaze had turned on the discovery of the escape? How long had it taken for him to begin watching the shadow for the merest hint of an out-of-place movement?

Had he read Jonas's mind, fathomed his thinking and come to the same conclusion: that a dark, deserted warehouse was the only hiding place? Was he out there now?

Jonas grunted to himself, ran his fingers over the butt of the holstered Colt and slipped silently from the shadowed main street with its growing bustle of bodies to the quieter, darker ground at the rear of the buildings.

He wended his way through the clutter of lean-to shelters, shacks and outbuildings, taking care to keep the quayside, the slow curl of smoke from the *Ada Benson's* stack and the comings and goings of the men refuelling her clear in his view, then paused a moment before crossing the last few yards to the warehouse.

He had noticed nothing of the man following him.

Had Jonas turned he would have been certain to spot the lean, long-limbed fellow loping like some awkward animal in his wake; a fellow he had seen before, might have noted for his sharp features and fidgety fingers; one of Birdboy's side-kicks.

The man had closed rapidly on Jonas as he approached the quay. Now, while Jonas peered ahead, his concentration fixed on the dark windows of the warehouse, the man reached for Jonas's neck, his fingers clawing for a hold.

Jonas spun round on the instinct of a threat, the Colt drawn and into his grip in seconds. The sidekick sneered, the momentum of surprise attack lost. He tried to step back, give himself space for another lunge, but Jonas's Colt was already swinging through its first lash, whipping across the man's cheek and jaw like an iron talon.

The man choked on a groan, fell back towards the shadows, another whipping swing of the gun barrel cracking across his temple. His eyes rolled, he bubbled saliva and slumped to a heap in the dirt of the alley.

'No bullet for you, fella,' murmured Jonas, dragging the body well out of sight. 'Can't spare one. Must be your lucky night.'

He licked at his sweat, holstered the Colt, and turned his attention back to the warehouse, the sweat turning to ice in his pores as he watched Birdboy emerge from the shadows to thud a boot into the building's main door fronting the quay, growl, shout a curse and set his levelled twin Colts blazing wildly.

TWENTY-TWO

Jonas sprang from the shadows like something launched, disregarding the sudden mayhem erupting round him as the shots roared across the night, intent only on reaching the warehouse before it filled with Calpott's men.

'What the hell's happenin' here?' yelled the sheriff, a mass of waving arms and thundering legs. He stumbled to a halt on the quay and roared his orders. 'That Birdboy there? Somebody go help him, f'Cris'sake. You – get over to the saloon, raise Zackman. You – get to Mr Wensum, tell him looks like Birdboy's found the woman. And you – watch for that Jonas fella. Where the hell's he hidin'?'

A man turning from Calpott tripped, reached to gain his balance, sent an empty crate crashing from its stack into a pile of barrels which rolled under the feet of the men scattering to the sheriff's orders.

'In hell's name, will you look where you're goin' there!' fumed Calpott, his arms like boughs in a wind. 'Watch it! Will somebody get—' A rolling barrel crashed into his shins to send him sprawling in a groan of curses.

'There's a fella out cold, and bleedin' like a hog back here,' yelled a man from the alley.

Barrels rolled, crates crashed. Men shouted. Calpott's orders were lost in the crack and roar of Birdboy's blazing Colts.

Jonas skidded to a halt in the warehouse, banged the door shut behind him and latched it tight, then moved into a suddenly tensed, tight silence.

'Step right on, Mr Jonas,' sneered Birdboy from the shadows. 'I got you covered, so I'll deal with you first.'

Jonas peered into the darkness where he recalled the stairs to the upper storey to be. Nothing of Furneaux or Alicia; no sight, no sound. He turned slowly to the grating tone of Birdboy's voice.

'Well, now, ain't we just covered some ground between us, Mr Jonas? Why, if I didn't figure you for bein' so damned law-abidin' deep down and so smitten to that banker's daughter's good looks, I might fancy havin' you my side of the fence. How about that, eh? Some team we could've made.'

Birdboy chuckled above the chaos still erupting on the quayside, then hawked and spat impatiently.

'But we ain't got the time for contemplatin' all that, have we?' he went on. 'Too much at stake, Mr Jonas, too much to play for. A big pot, eh? So here's my deal: you get the chance to leave here alive and make it best you can out of town, nobody on your tail, nobody trackin' you, and I get the woman and the safe passage Wensum, Zackman and myself are needin' downriver. What yuh say? It a deal?'

'Zackman's dead.' said Jonas flatly. 'He ain't goin' no place.'

Calpott's voice echoed. Footfalls thudded along boardwalks. Somebody began banging on the warehouse door. The sheriff's orders silenced him.

'You been busy, Mr Jonas,' drawled Birdboy before spitting again. 'So we lost Zackman. T'ain't no fuss. The deal still stands.'

Jonas shifted gently, silently, his eyes aching with the strain of peering into the shadows for the gunslinger, shifting to probe the deeper darkness for a hint of Alicia and her father.

A new quiet began to settle on the quayside. Calpott had stopped shouting. Men were no longer running. Somewhere a dog howled to leave a long echo.

'I'm waitin' on you, Mr Jonas,' piped Birdboy.

Jonas moved again, praying that his boot did not ease to one of the many creaky floorboards, sighing softly when the boot was steady again and the board unmoved.

'I'm countin' you down to three on this,' said Birdboy irritably. 'And startin' now. One . . . Two. . . .'

Jonas licked his lips, tasted the hot, salty sweat, drew his Colt carefully, and took the gamble in one flying leap for the foot of the stairs.

'Three!'

Birdboy's twin Colts raged like sudden torches, revealing his position in the shadows to the left.

Jonas hit the stairs with a sickening thud, rolled, let the gun roar wildly and without aim, but with enough venom to silence Birdboy for the few seconds it took to scramble into new cover.

'Yuh just bein' a blind fool there, yuh hear?' snapped Birdboy. 'T'ain't goin' to do you no good. You've had this comin' since that night at the shack. Should've put an end to you long back. Still, always the best at the last, eh? Same as it'll be when I finally get to that woman up there.'

The Colts blazed again. Jonas shrank to the deeper cover.

'Ain't no place to hide, fella.'

He was probably right at that, thought Jonas, squirming away to his right, listening for the sound of Birdboy's steps, watching for the glint of a gun barrel, still wondering where Alicia and her father had buried themselves.

Another blaze, this time accompanied by a chuckle. 'Gettin' to be somethin' of a hunt, ain't it, Mr Jonas? But one I ain't really got the time for right now.'

Jonas winced and bit at his lip as the next roar skimmed a sliver of flesh from his gun hand, sending his Colt sliding across the floor. 'Hell!' he mouthed, sucking at the damaged hand, then scrambling madly for the knife sheathed in his belt.

'This just ain't your night, mister,' grinned Birdboy, stepping closer to become a stark silhouetted shape, the Colts ranged and steadied for the final blaze. 'And you can forget the knife. You'd be dead before your fingers bent to it.' His grin twitched at one corner and began to fade. 'Sorry about this, fella. Like I say, we could've made one helluva team—'

The Winchester roared to a blistering, shuddering echo that rolled round the warehouse like the fire-breath of an enraged beast.

Jonas cringed and blinked on the rage and the repeat that crashed in its wake from the top of the stairs. He watched Birdboy's arms drop to his sides, the Colts clatter to the floor, his eyes widen in a glazed look of astonishment, the blood begin to soak through his shirt like an oozing pool of the Big Muddy.

It seemed to Jonas then that the man was suspended in time and space for a long, chilling minute, but it was only seconds before Birdboy crashed face-down and twitched only once in the still oozing blood beneath him.

Jonas was at the foot of the stairs as Alicia, her father a step behind her, descended slowly, almost mesmerically, the still-smoking Winchester clutched in her left hand.

'I ain't never seen. . . I never thought, not in my wildest dreams. . .' spluttered Furneaux, the sweat glistening like ice on his brow.

Jonas reached to take the rifle, then to guide Alicia from the last steps where she paused a moment, her eyes round and staring, the merest tremble at her lips, before slipping gladly into his arms.

'What the hell is happening, Sheriff ?' insisted Harley Wensum, his face wet with sweat, tight with concern, as he glared at the darkened warehouse and then at Calpott. 'Get some men in there, f'Cris'sake. Who's doin the shooting?'

'The men ain't keen to go chasin' in Birdboy's steps,' flustered Calpott. 'The fella ain't for rilin', not in a situation like this. 'Sides, Zackman's been knifed to death.'

Wensum glowered and stiffened. 'Zackman's no loss now. Damn it, it's the woman we want.'

'My boys are beginnin' to spook,' said Calpott, as if unaware of Wensum. 'That Jonas fella's been prowlin'. They ain't certain who's goin' to be next to fall foul of him, not if—'

'Tell them I'll double their pay,' snapped Wensum. 'Tell them any damned thing you like, only get them moving. Or do I have to get in there myself?'

'I wouldn't do that if I were you, Mr Wensum,' shrugged the sheriff. 'In fact—'

'Then torch the place!' stormed Wensum. 'Burn it to the ground!'

A bull-chested man turned from the gathering facing the building. 'Ain't no way you can do that, mister,' he quipped confidently. 'Folks livin' round here depend on the quay. That warehouse goes up and we'd lose the boat trade out of Fort Bragg.' His chest expanded on a deep breath. 'No, mister, can't be done. *Won't* be done!'

The men around him murmured their agreement. 'See what I mean, Mr Wensum?' gestured Calpott. 'Town ain't for a torchin' – and neither am I. You're goin' to have to think of somethin' else.'

'I already have,' fumed Wensum. 'Give me a gun. Any gun. Just give it to me!'

'I'd think twice about what you have in mind, Mr Wensum,' said the sheriff, drawing his own loaded Colt from its holster and handing it to him.

'There's been some shootin' in there; a Colt, and then a Winchester. But there's been nothin' since the rifle shots, which suggests to me—'

'Give me the gun, man, and cut the belly-aching!' blustered Wensum, snatching the weapon from Calpott. 'We are wasting time here.'

He turned on a spinning heel and strode across the cluttered quay, the gun tight in his grip, his gaze fixed like a beam on the warehouse. He muttered irritably through each step, sweat gleaming on his cheeks, his immaculately frilled shirt-front stained with the lingering drift of smoke from the *Ada Benson*, his tailored coat crumpled and dirt-smudged.

He halted in front of the warehouse, gazed over the darkened windows, the closed door, and raised his voice in a single call. 'Birdboy – you get out here right now, or I'm coming in.' He waited a moment. 'You hear me?' he called again. 'I am not for wasting another minute—'

The door to the warehouse opened wide and suddenly creaked and scraped to a standstill and for a moment presented a dark, gaping mouth to the wide-eyed Harley Wensum.

It was a full ten seconds before the blood-stained body of Birdboy was spewed from the black hole to the quay.

Wensum stared, new sweat beading his already lathered face, his mind reeling for a moment, limbs lifeless and remote. He raised his eyes slowly to gaze into the tight, expressionless face of Jonas straddling the threshold to the warehouse behind him, the Winchester gripped in his now loosely bound injured hand.

'You, damn you,' he mouthed, the Colt hanging loose at his side. 'Jonas-whoever-you-are.' His eyes narrowed. He licked at hot sweat. 'I want that woman, and I want her now. You hear me, mister? I said *now*, and that's what I mean. Get her!'

Jonas said nothing, did not move.

Sheriff Calpott swallowed, fingered the gap of his empty holster, glanced quickly at the men around him and began slowly, self-consciously to sidle away to the shadows.

'Yuh ain't pullin' out on us now, are you, Sheriff?' sneered the bull-chested man, stepping to block Calpott's way. 'Things are just about to get real interestin', I'd say, wouldn't you?'

The sheriff smiled thinly and stood still.

'Well?' grated Wensum, his voice seeming to crawl on all-fours from the depths of his throat. 'I trust I am not wasting my breath here, am I? You just bring that woman I'm set to wed to my side. I've been missing her.' The sweat on his face bubbled feverishly. 'You can shoot the old man. He is of no further use. Him and his bank can go to hell! Tell him that.' He grinned. 'Better still I'll tell him myself. Stand aside there!'

Jonas stood his ground.

'I said shift,' yelled Wensum.

Jonas did not so much as blink.

'You will not be asked again. This time—'

Wensum had raised the Colt, released a single shot, high and wide, blinked on his sweat, growled, and levelled the gun again, when Jonas steadied the Winchester and let it roar across the night, throwing Wensum back like river flotsam to the boards of the quay where he did not move again.

'Sonofa-goddamn-bitch,' mouthed Calpott.

'Yeah,' murmured the bull-chested man, 'he was all of that, sure enough.'

TWENTY-THREE

'Cripple Creek is destined for big things, and I am personally goin' to see it achieves every one of them: proper law and order for decent folk goin' about earnin' an honest livin'; a bigger quayside for the expandin' river trade; more stores, new livery and, not least, a bank. Yessir, a very special branch of the St Louis and Illinois State Bank.'

Oliver Furneaux grew expansive, smiling and generous behind a thick cloud of cigar smoke, strode deliberately across the saloon bar of the Palace Hotel to a framed parchment map of the Big Muddy, and tapped a finger at the point marked Cripple Creek.

'Here, gentlemen,' he announced, 'is where we are. Ten years from now this will be one of the leading, if not the most important, towns east of Montana territory.' He turned in a swirl of smoke to the assembled gathering of town men and women. 'That is my prediction; that is what I'm ready to help you folk work towards, and that is what I'm standin' by.'

There was a long murmuring of approval and a smattering of applause.

'Mighty generous of you, Mr Furneaux,' said the tall clean-shaven spokesman for the gathering, 'and I speak here for everybody when I say we're grateful, 'specially after the events of these past days. Not a deal for Cripple Creek to be proud of and that's for sure, but with Sheriff Calpott and most of his sidekicks under lock and key awaiting the arrival of the marshal from Fort Bragg, and them gunslingers of Zackman's and Birdboy's scattered to the wind, well, we mebbe really do have a future worth lookin' to. But, heck, it was a close run thing there!'

'You can say that again, fella,' beamed Furneaux through more smoke, 'but we made it. The gold is still safely aboard the *Ada Benson* and Captain McBright tells me we'll be castin' off for St Louis come noon today. I'll be back here to see how things are goin' in just a month.'

'What about your daughter, Mr Furneaux?' asked a woman anxiously. 'She had a rough time out there.'

'She's restin' up aboard the *Ada Benson* right now, ma'am, but I'm grateful to you for askin', and she'll be real touched at your concern.' Furneaux gestured with a cigar. 'But she'll be back. You can bet to that, ma'am. I know my daughter, and believe me she's some gal. Yessir, she'll be back.'

'And that fella they called Jonas,' said a man from the back of the gathering, 'what about him? Ain't seen a sight of him since the night of the shootin'.'

'Gone,' said Furneaux bluntly. 'Just that, mister – gone. Disappeared. Rode out of here before first light that very mornin', and there's been no word

of him since. Pity, because we all of us owe him a
great deal, includin' our very lives in some
instances, and me more than most.'

He turned back to the parchment map of the
Big Muddy. 'My only guess,' he murmured
thoughtfully,' is that he's somewhere out there;
somewhere along the banks of the Big Muddy. . . .'

Jonas patted the mount's neck, drew carefully on
the cheroot and narrowed his gaze on the movement along the banks of the river far below him.

Tracking Cheyenne, he mused; four of Eagle
Neck's bucks scouting out the morning's flotsam
for whatever it might yield. Not a deal, he reckoned, watching the ponies pick their way deli-
cately among the rocks and pebbled inlets. River
trade was still not brisk. Be another month yet
before it reached its peak; time enough, he
figured, for him to be long clear of the territory
and high into the last of the snowline.

The plains of Montana in six weeks, he smiled
to himself, and the warm winds of open country to
follow for as long as the mood held to him.

He drew on the cheroot again, watched the
smoke loop a pine bough, and grunted quietly, his
thoughts clouding on the night in Cripple Creek,
the long shadows, blood, death, bodies; the sight of
the sweating, twitching, gold-crazed Harley
Wensum, the roar and blaze of guns. . .the feel of
Alicia Furneaux safe in his arms.

Times past, he reckoned. He had done no more,
no less than any fellow would have in the circumstances. The Furneaux would resolve their own
fates, the folk of Cripple Creek find their own way,

rid of the bad blood of the likes of Birdboy and Zackman.

Captain McBright would take charge of his steamer once again and the *Ada Benson* continue to ply her trade through all the vagaries of the sweep of the Big Muddy.

But, damn it, he never had got to that apple pie and night's sleep in clean sheets on a decent bed!

He took a last look at the trailing Cheyenne bucks, doused the cheroot and reined the mount round sharply to the track through the pines to the bluff's main trail to the high north-west.

And it was in those next few seconds that he first heard the scuff of the approaching rider and then saw her face-on through the web of branches.

'What the—? he blustered, reining back into a clutter of twigs and fronds.

'Mr Jonas,' smiled Alicia, easing her mount a step closer. 'I thought I might have missed you.'

Jonas pulled his hat back into position. 'Missed me? Since when were you lookin' for me, ma'am? I thought—'

'I know, I know, you thought, and rightly so, that I would be heading back with my father aboard the *Ada Benson* to all the comforts of St Louis. And so I was, until I woke this morning.'

Alicia's gaze settled warmly on Jonas's face. 'Wouldn't work, though, would it? Not after all that happened down there on the river, back at Cripple Creek, and especially not after. . .after Harley.' Her eyes glazed for a moment, then she tossed her hair decisively. 'No, Mr Jonas, St Louis is no longer for me nor I for it.'

'That's all very well, ma'am, but the sort of alternative you look as if you're thinkin' about. . . .'

'Warm shirt, buckskin pants, stout boots, and spares back there in the packhorse I'm trailing. And only two dresses packed – just in case.' She winked and smiled again. 'Oh, and a Winchester and ammunition. Good enough?'

'Good enough for what, ma'am?' frowned Jonas.

'For travellin' with you up country to wherever it is you're going.'

'But I'm not sure—'

'Neither am I, but I am more than ready and willing to give it a go, Mr Jonas. Captain McBright back there was kind enough and understanding enough to help me with all I needed, including the horses, and I've left a long note of explanation to my pa. He'll be upset to begin with, but, being Oliver Furneaux, he'll recover and we'll keep contact, pa will ensure to that. Meanwhile—'

'Meanwhile, ma'am, I don't think you have any real notion of just what it is you're gettin' yourself into here. If you're figurin'—'

'Hungry Cheyenne bucks, gold and women-crazed gunslingers, canoes, storms, flooded rivers, being held prisoner for ransom, a two-bit, sonofabitch, double-dealing fellow scheming to rob my father and marry me. . . If there's more, Mr Jonas, you can tell me about it as we make our way to. .. to where exactly?'

Jonas sighed. 'I was plannin' on Montana, ma'am.'

'Montana sounds just fine to me,' smiled Alicia. 'Oh, and if you're at all concerned about the

Cheyenne, a buck who looked very much to me like Eagle Neck himself watched me for a long while from up there on the south-facing knoll and then seemed to wave me on. Is that a good sign, Mr Jonas? Perhaps it's a lucky omen. . . .'